Passengers

Archie Aston

Copyright © 2014 by Archie Aston
All rights reserved. This book or any portion thereof may not be reproduced or used in any manner whatsoever without the express written permission of the publisher except for the use of brief quotations in a book review.

Printed in Germany

First Printing, 2014

ISBN 978-1-291-97712-7

Cover Photo by Tessa Ayling-Guhl
Back Cover Photo by Gearoid Seoighe

Cover Design by Michael Dennery
Book Design by Gerhard Weiß

CONTENTS

CUNEIFORM	7
IMAGING	17
NOTES	27
COLLEAGUES	43
ESCAPE	57
OWNERSHIP	73
UNREST	89
REST	125

CUNEIFORM

I care too much what other people think. About what they think about me.

Another truth unlocked as I lie here on this hospital bed.

I can walk now, but I prefer to do my thinking lying down, staring up at the panels of the ceiling, wondering how many people had had the same view as they slipped into death.

I've started to narrate my life, to help with my writing. The nurse greets me with a clinical good morning, she looks like she's been up all night, and she probably has. She has no time for short talk. She slips the syringe into the meatus of my cock as I inhale like a victim and keep my eyes on those panels. A short time passes before she feeds the catheter down down down into me. That kind of thing.

A prison might be anywhere one doesn't want to be, but I'm feeling quite happy to be here. I wish the circumstances were different, and my jaw wasn't wired, and my arm not broken, and my insides so beaten up that I can't take a piss. But sometimes, before, when I was walking to work, I'd hope to be hit by a car as I crossed the road. I would not look left or right and keep my tired eyes on the tarmac and wait for the hit. I would be sent to a quiet hospital ward somewhere to embark on a slow and peaceful recovery. So I guess I got what I wanted, although it might have been a lot easier if I was hit by a car.

Either way I have this time to think and read and write and that's all I ever wanted. Now I can tell the story of how I got here.

I acquired an easel from one of the therapy wards and use that as my desk now, writing standing up when I have the strength, standing back and seeing the words from a distance like a water colour. My memory has always been most excited by colours. For some people it's smells, faces or a voice. For me it has always been colour, the deepest sordid vermillion or the stained cream of blue cheese, colours and context in union. Unfortunately, there is a time in my life which is woven immutably with the grey black of a deep winter dusk and the black grey of a deep winter dawn. It feels like two years without sunlight.

I was rising at five in the morning, from monday to friday before work, and dragging myself to my kitchen table and sitting in front of my computer to write my book. Sometimes I'd get a couple of hours in before rushing off to work for eight AM. Sometimes I'd fall right back asleep on the keys, pasting

the buttons with drool and writing nothing but
8IM777777777777777777 . But mostly I'd stare vacantly at the screen, admiring the virgin page.

You woke me up again this morning, she'd tell me when I faded back in from work. I'd say sorry with a ritual vacuity. I'd see a crispy mountain of dishes in the sink over her shoulder and wonder what time she got out of bed. She'd tell me they're just soaking and keep me on topic; so how's this book coming along? Have you nearly finished it yet?
It's coming along.
That was my standard fabrication. Did you get chance to read the chapter I printed for you?
No not yet, will do later though, don't wait up, mwah.

And then she would be gone, most likely to the gym where she'd spend hours becoming taut and distant. She'd leave me to collapse on the sofa surrounded by her clothes and things. I could usually force a carton of wine down me, tranquillised on the sofa, writhing sporadically to unwind my clogged muscles.

The telly would blur away in front of me, dragging me down to its level. It was one of those nights of the calendar year that the rich turn up and implore us to pick up our phones and throw some money at problems. Some comic relief. They torture us with their painless peach faces as they go serious and introduce us to the cast of victims we can pepper with gold tonight. They offer us redemption from our armchair guilt, as we hide behind our fatuity asking questions to the screen like how could these things happen in the world? They hide in their habits like priests, invoking the collection plate and retail salvation. They tell us to pick up the phone.

They show us the tired faces of sub-Saharan Africa, the marginalised souls of refugee camps, thirsty ghosts desperate for what we take for granted. They show us the children of Gaza, punished for breathing and soaked in blood.

They show us an old man's life in photography, weddings and birthdays and trips to the beach bookended with super8. He's healthy, alive. All his smiles are in his wife's direction, and rightly so. She's grey before her time, but beautiful. A few home videos affirm her status as Mother, Partner and Lover, the holy trinity.

And then they show us him now, the survivor, wilted by the strains of completion, shrivelled and ending. He was dying alone.

His wife of the pictures and the home video, the grainy woman we'd been introduced to in the retrospective showreel was dead. Drowned slowly by Alzheimer's. They asked us to pick up our phones. Empty your wallets and we'll take him off your screen and you can go back to your usual programs tomorrow.

We all die alone. That's what I tell the scared old man on the screen. We all die alone. My unheard advice, my comfort to deaf ears. I took my eyes off the screen and stared at the vanilla wall to it's right, lost in torment. I probably should be writing this all down I thought, as I slipped blindly into my daily coma.

Dreams are futile to anyone other than their beholders, as personal as pride and private parts. But that doesn't stop us from unravelling them to others, as if addressing them will keep them alive, like we have a choice in the matter. Dreams are unstable by their nature and easily forgotten, but we treatise them all the same.

Mine had me sat atop a gigantic salty tongue. I could feel the kingsize organ waggle with anticipation as I realised it's width. I felt the sulphuric breath of the black chasm behind me. 100's of thin teeth arced around me, topping mammoth gums, like snow capping an impenetrable peninsula. Stalactite replicas reflected above. I stared up at the vast pink roof, and a chant echoed off it, bouncing around the cavernous mouth of the whale. If I was not mistaken, it was one of those first songs on The Dark Side of the Moon, Speak To Me, or Breathe.

I fell back into reality as I prepared for engulfment, as if closing my eyes in the dream had opened them outside of it. My hair was stuck to the side of my face with slobber and my face was stuck to a faux leather pillow. I reached for the wine carton and shook it to judge its use. A courteous splosh indicated I was in, and so I poured its end into my stained beaker.

The nap had rejuvenated me enough to sit up, and turn the telly off. I felt I should seize the moment, make use of the peace and space and relative freedom, the wine pushing me in the right direction at least. I staggered over to my desk and the computer like it was five in the morning.

And once again I admired the virgin page.

Essentially, I wanted to write a highbrow murder mystery, solid and original and twisted by intellectualism. I had a full notebook of ideas which craved breath and movement, narratives that traversed all dimensions. Concepts that eulogised the anecdote. But when I penned them out it felt as convoluted as growing up. I found another carton and tried to drink myself into the zone. I had my opening:

```
The Sun peered over the mountain and
thawed my face where I lay on the rock
returning from sleep.  I had crashed so
that means the ringing in my ears must
have stopped too.  I waited for it to
start up again as I watched the mist
relinquish the valley, leaving a beautiful
morning in its wake.  All would be  green
in the Valley of Lost Souls today.  And
the ringing had gone for now.  I
resettled on the rock and fled back to
sleep in the blanket of the Sun.
```

I had my set up:

```
A strident scream arrived in my ears
dragging me back to the light and the
rock.  There it was again, awful and
distant.  But it wasn't in my own head.
It came once again over the brow, this
time even more desperate. I peeled myself
```

from the rock and the blanket of the Sun
and headed to the lake to investigate,
tired but content.

The lake was secret and high in the
mountains. The water ran down from the
rocks all around, as clean as it was cold
and rousing. I was above it looking down
at it's crystal stillness, feeling lucky
to know it. How could a scream so
terrible come from such a place?

I could make out four figures down near
the waters edge, the mist still lurking
around them. I scrambled down, as rushed
as I had ever been since I moved to these
parts. The Sun had yet to reach this
slope and as soon as I embarked down it I
felt an ominous chill.

I had my murder scene:

When I got down to the lake I regarded the
mist to be far more ubiquitous and heavy
than I had expected. There were shapes in
the fog, fingers and halos and animals
and the like, although they'd always
dissipate before my tired brain could
catch up with my impatient eye, only
something deep inside me had seen them.
And there I came across the four figures I
had seen from above, all dressed like me
as we all did, in our animal hides.

Except for one, who was lying on the ground, naked.

I could see now that she was dead, as peaceful as she was a cool pale purple. All stared upon her and my entrance was not acknowledged.

I recognised her face now, her beautiful dead face. It was Kyra.

'What happened here?' I asked quietly.
'She has flown brother. She has flown' choked Martha, who was holding herself together with her own arms.
'I'm sorry' I choked back. I knew they were close. And lovers too.
'I screamed for help, but she had already flown. I can't... I can't believe it.'
I believed her.

Phillip and Damo were the other two figures. They were both statues either side of the scene, Phillip full of sadness, and Damo reverentially stoic. Nobody said anything for sometime. Martha choked some more, hidden partially in the mist. And I suddenly realised that Martha wasn't Kyra's only lover stood there.

I consoled myself with the opinion that it was an OK start. But it only took the micro-event of the first glass from the fresh carton to realise it was all I had to offer that virgin page. I held a beautiful starting gun in my hand, but it was a paper tiger. A sanitary replica.

I sought solace in the world wide web and a new cup of wine. I had one more exercise to resort to, a ceremony of circumvention that wouldn't let my free house go to waste. I couldn't write but at least I could wank. I started off on the Craigslist personals, looking for people more lonely than I.

kick me in the balls m4m (26)
Want fun with fat (39)
in search of a hard mouthfucker for my slave w4m (26)
Sexy transvestite looking for the same t4t (25)
Fuck My Cum Out Of My Cock (35)
Wanking Partner (37)
Woman likes younger men with smelly underwear w4mm (36)
sissy looking for some one to take pictures (35)
Virgin looking for some fun w4m (22)
want to give first bj and be treated like a slut RIGHT NOW (25)
Dominant East-Asian guy wanted! w4m (35)
Can you drain me? m4w (34)

I browsed all of the loneliest people the night could offer me, reading their frantic pleas, beasting over their pixelated shots of tits and cocks and stockings and shaved pussy and balls and lipstick and cum. I took my weapon into the palm of my hand

and spat down upon it. No wonder this is the most popular thing on the Internet.

Then it would be time to get myself worked up on the professionals. The amateur always held a special place on the palate of my pudenda, but exoticism is a potent hardener. To this day I have never fucked an american for that reason, I wouldn't want to hear YES FUCK MY FUCKING ASSHOLE or FUCK ME FUCK ME DADDY or DON'T FUCKING STOP FUCK ME FUCKING HARDER coming out of something real with an accent, something palpable, other than the tinny grunts of my computer speaker. I don't want to find fissures in that licensed fantasy.

I polished myself like an ornament. I demented myself, impetuous to see how deep the rabbit hole plunged. I was under the adolescent spell we pretend we grow out of, and nothing else mattered till I came. I was fully compromised when she came home early through the door.

I slammed the laptop shut but the groans and the splats and the swearing still played from the speakers and they wouldn't stop.

No matter. She had seen enough.

IMAGING

We stood uneasily in the sterile nave of the museum, skimming the information placards, shocked by their banality. A nazi propaganda poster hung before me, an artefact from the celluloid age, dragged through the slime of time, doubtful to be dug up in a far away future like their stone, iron and bronze cousins we'd just passed. But I thought at least it was tangible. What will they hang in the museum walls on our digital age? An approximation of the email which ignited world war three?

He looks fat, she said as she sniffed at the fascist model on the poster. He held an axe in his arm and was indeed topless. He was strapping and robust and heroically handsome. He was a picture of health and enterprise and progress. He was juxtaposed with a picture of a disabled boy, physically, and with whom stance and circumstance implied a mental affliction to boot. A jingle for eugenics read out beneath, in that gorgeous germanic font the narrow part of my mind identifies as evil, like the reds and the blacks it's written in.

He isn't fat, I nearly said back, but she'd moved on, heading unashamedly closer to the exit.

The placard spoke to me like it was bored. Action T4 was Nazi Germany's euthanasia programme during which physicians murdered over 250,000 people judged to be unfit to live on the basis of racial hygiene the poster above was used in the media to propagate ideas on racial cleansing and sterilisation to the masses before the majority of murders happened in secret and.

I shook my head stoically to stave off the sickness, my hangover rekindled by the evil.

They showed me cruelly cramped pictures of pictures. Beautiful work from a legion of tortured artists, judged incapable of contributing to pure society. Painters and writers and creators sterilised and then murdered. I thought about my book and how I didn't get up early enough this morning.

I stared back at the blonde and blue eyed propaganda man, half naked post labour, the proud belly of fascism. I'd seen his great grandson on our way to the museum, exploded onto the side of a double decker bus in full and false colour. His distant son seized no axe, and pervaded a different kind of eroticism in his toplessness. He looked happier to be an advert anyway, and that was his labour.

I had stared at his freakish six pack and inexplicably wide shoulders and teeth as white as Hiroshima's blitz and had wondered how much of his life he'd wasted to get them. The window framed faces of the normals stared down from inside the tall bus, a collective misery, maybe unaware a fantasy pec or ab sat blown up next to them.

I thought of the vacancy of their commute as I studied the twisted fingers of the severely disabled young man sat in the nazi hogwash, the proud axe man's counterpart and enemy. He was a photo of genetic uselessness, a failure of god.

Just think Goebbels used to force this shit down people's throats at great expense, dropping it out of planes and so on. How proud he would be of today, so eager are we for our daily dose of deceit, and paying cash money for it too. He'd see us grab a handful of backbiting and backslapping on our rush to work from the newsagents. And he'd see us rush back from work to watch some more. We are Goebbels conceited delight, I guess.

Can we go now, she asked, entering the gift shop. We hadn't spoken much about what she saw the other night, what she had caught me up to, my familiarity with depravity. Her exposure to my private world of masturbation. She had chosen the carrot rather than the whip to keep us plodding forward, that silent root vegetable in the room. I took the bait, keeping quiet too so we could stumble on.

```
I looked at Martha and then Phillip, their
eyes still locked on the corpse. I looked
at Damo and now he was looking at me and
we approached each other  silently.  He
```

took me a few steps away so we could not
be over heard. He spoke to me with
checked stealth.
'This doesn't look good' he said.
'I know. That poor girl, poor Kyra.
What shall we do now? We need to find out
what happened.'
'We do, we do brother. But we also need
to take care of our good sister, take her
back to the Pile. She should be with our
people now.'
'Do you not think we should go to the
village?'
'Certainly not. She was one of us, she is
none of their concern, and she never will
be. They're not like us, don't you
remember? They have no respect for their
dead, or their living for that matter.
Don't you remember?'
'Yes I remember.'

The village was thirty miles away, the
nearest remnant of the society we had all
left behind. It was an isolated outpost, a
last outcrop of cruel civilisation, with
the towns and the cities we'd all ran from
far beyond it. But it still had enough
of human kind to render us as enemies. In
years gone by we would sometimes travel
there to try and trade, but the last time
we had taken that silk road they had made
it very clear we would not be welcomed
again. They stole everything we had taken
there and we were fortunate to get back

to the Pile alive. They beat us while their women and children watched, they took the animal hides from our backs and drove us out, making us walk back into the wilderness naked, freezing and abject.

'This certainly doesn't look good' I concurred again.
'I take it you've noticed the marks around her neck.'
'Yes I've seen.'
'This was no accident.'
'I know my brother. I am very scared to say I know.'

Martha was now covering the corpse with her natural blanket and lying down next to her and sobbing. Phillip still stood watching, unable to stop. I couldn't say if they too had noticed the ligature points on her neck, the bruising, the bite marks and the blood around her mouth and nostril. But it wasn't likely, they didn't used to be cops, unlike Damo and I. In our past lives.

'We should do a search of the area, retrace her movements and see if the lake holds any secrets' I said, still whispering.
'You sound like your old self brother. And you know already that this lake holds many secrets. Secrets we aren't at liberty to disturb.'
'There's been a murder here Damo. We can

both see that.'
'And we will not let truth escape us. But now we must respect and honour our sister. We must get her back to the Pile.'

Over the years I had found many ways to not think about my past life, before I found myself in this beautiful land, in the Valley of Lost Souls. It wasn't a form of escape from my memories, as I used to do back in the city, through fucking and drink and movies and drugs. We had none of those things at the Pile, well, we called it neighbouring not fucking. And we were all neighbours here.

And we didn't dodge and desert our memories, we confronted them, we sat down with them and travelled with them and we scrutinised them and we made them our friends. That way we could say goodbye to them forever. But what I was seeing now, what I was thinking now, meant something had returned from somewhere deep down. Something had surfaced for one more feverish dance, like the reappearance of some looped childhood nightmare. My beautiful sister had flown and all I could think was SCENE, EVIDENCE, SUSPECTS.

It was harder for me and Damo too, having come together, a couple. It was harder to say goodbye to our old selves when we had been our old selves together. The others

saw us as a pair and it took along time
for them to forget that.

We wouldn't allow it now of course. You
must always come alone, it's as close as
we have to a rule or maxim. We don't have
too many others, our principles usually
defined by our collective difficulty with
civilisation.

But it helped that we were in the First
Fifteen, and times have changed here at
the Pile, here in the Valley of Lost
Souls.

A cup of coffee gone cold sat still next to me, a milky grey like the light which slipped through the curtains and onto my desk. My eyes were open but I had slipped back into the realm of the dream, so lucid was that world where I had found myself, in the luminous mouth of whale once again. I recounted it once again as my eyes glazed over, my hand frozen with the useless pen jailed inside it.

I had slipped down the throat of the whale with little fuss, rushed on by the salty water. I splashed down and dropped into the great cavern that was the whale's tummy. It felt like being ankle deep in a swamp, inside a giant military hangar, the size of which the blackness made impossible to ever know. The air was salty and warm, but the stench was not as bad as you'd think, it was quite comforting really. As was Pink Floyd, which had never stopped playing, but now seemed to be pumped over a Tannoy address system dotted around the rafters atop the great hall of the stomach. I fumbled myself to my feet, and stretched my arms out into the darkness, as if looking for a light switch. I felt only dank air, and so inched a small step in an instinctive direction, but froze when confronted by a terrible avian hissing. The hiss was loud and visceral, more so than the record which floated above, channelled through the tinny speakers. And then another hiss, animated by the first, rose from just behind, deeper and with added venom. I felt the shuffling of many many feathered bodies around me.

I attempted a murmur, if only to deprecate my predicament, something like a guttural 'Shit'. But no sound came forward. I expected a panic to set hold, as the deafening bells and clocks of Time now rang out, their hypnotic chaos only slightly diluted by the public address system. But the waves of panic were not forthcoming, maybe they were breaking on the gargantuan hulk of my Leviathan host, and I was safely stowed inside. Another territorial hiss cut the tense air around me, urging me to reconsider. I was sure I felt something peck my ankle, strong like a warning.

The trance was ended by the stabs of my alarm clock, reminding me it was time for real work, my early morning session drowned in those greys and blacks, and delivered a rude retirement. I tried desperately to remember my Goebbels line, but all I could think about was the belly of the whale, and the cash registers and the crazy man's laughter and the hurtling bass, and guitars breaking loose like a series of unbelievable dawns. I was Jonah on The Dark Side of the Moon. I thought about yesterday and how it felt like an injured day dream. My one day off in the museum, my one day off to recover. It was not enough.

NOTES

Imagine me with a model. A real life model. Well, I was. Five minutes after meeting her I was terrified of losing her, as soon as she slammed me against a wall and laid those lips on me, her hand grabbing cock balls and jeans all in one go. This is mine now, she whispered into my ear.

I slowly became a fiend, anything for those long legs, that sculpted arse and those huge eyes. Did I know then that those eyes were the only deep things about her? I was overpowered that's for sure.

We used to spend afternoons fucking drenched in sweat and slime only stopping to get higher. Her house was falling down and she was the only one living in it, a big old Georgian fucker, completely dilapidated. I'm not sure she was supposed to be in there. But we had no neighbours to bother as we fucked our way through the ruins and the debris and the chaos. By winter she'd moved into mine.

I used to think she liked me having a go at the writing. Your stuff's really good you should send it off she'd say, as I shrugged and looked at her naked and smoking and damp. But now it seems to annoy her, a bad habit I'll drop when I finally finish.

```
I took Kyra's dead legs and Damo took the
torso under her armpits. Martha and
Phillip flanked offering their sombre
support and our cheerless cortege headed
back to the Pile. It was not a long
journey, mainly upwards and soon we were
out of the mist and we could see our home
in the distance clinging to the
mountaintop.

Fires had already been lit or else
sustained from the night before and their
illegible signals ran high into the
morning blue. There was an ancient and
crumbled sheep housing there, the only
stone building of our commune. It was in
that long abandoned hostel that the First
Fifteen stayed on that fateful night, when
```

the mountain weather became severe and iron-handed. It was there we sheltered and neighboured to stay warm and alive, as merciless winds and all genres of rain came down to teach us a lesson. And it was there in the luminous clarity of the following morning we decided to make our new home. I will never forget looking at Damo and the others there in that halcyon void, it felt like the first time I'd ever heard silence. An unbelievable energy moved me, a new faith had been found.

We were all affected by an eruption of productivity. Us First Fifteen working like we'd never worked before, for weeks and months and years, working for ourselves and for each other. We built the Pile, slowly and thwarted by fatigue and calamity and sometimes sorrow, but we built it. Other wanderers began to trickle into our fold, other self evacuees from progress sent running to the mountains by their despair. Our Pile grew and grew with every new accidental pilgrim.

We never wanted tourists so we never let word get back to the cities and the towns and the villages about our whereabouts and who we were and what we were doing. The people who found us had no idea we were there. They just knew they had to get away, to escape to the mountains and like a bug to the light they found us. We've not turned anyone away, yet.

A small party must have sensed the cavalcade of grief heading up hill and headed down to meet us, words and tears and screams were exchanged, people ran back and forth as we continued into the Pile and towards that old stone sheep shed we called the Pedestal. The drums had started up as we got there, the deep tribal rhythms rising and the throng of our brothers and sisters weeping for Kyra, her body risen by many mourning hands.

I knew what was coming and I wanted to move fast, so I let the hands take the body and I looked in the crowd for Damo. He still held her shoulders, pushing her up into the sky and carrying her to the clearing in front of the Pedestal. They had already started building the bonfire. The deep drone of the drums propelled the ritual.

'We need to tell them what's happened Damo. We need to let them know she hasn't flown naturally. We need more time with the body' I half whispered half shouted into his ear.
'We will my brother we will' he said with an absence that surprised me.
'We need to stop them then Damo. Help me.'
'Slow down brother' he said, now looking at me and letting the other hands carry Kyra on. He took my shoulders in his hands. He was lucidly stern.
'You're beginning to sound like your old

self. I can see those ghosts in your eyes, you know we can't let them come back to haunt us. We'll get to the bottom of this, but first we need to honour our sister. She may not have flown naturally but she has still flown. We owe her this brother you know that. You know that.'

I thought I knew Damo was right, but something clawed beneath and wouldn't let go. A galvanic ache began to take hold. And a lapsed nerve told me that I used to fall in love with that feeling; that chilling enigma, invigorating and dangerous. And maybe I was falling for it again. Kyra's sullied corpse had ensconced my being.

I chose not to pursue it verbally as Damo eyeballed me one last time and returned to the ritual at hand, the flames and drums and the black black smoke taken away on the mountain breeze.

You woke me up again this morning.
I forced a sorry through a yawn.
Good day at the office?

Meh I shrugged. Yours?
Good thank you. I've been very productive.
I raised an out of sight eyebrow as I filled the kettle at the sink.
Go on.
I've been a very busy bee. I've started on a new idea for an exhibition.
An artist now?
No, not *now*. Again.
An artist again?
Go fuck yourself she said with a sarcy smile and a dummy punch.

That last comment could have gone either way and I felt pretty lucky. I skinned up on the sofa and listened to her idea as she pottered around guiltily, looking busy. The idea sounded sound enough, a photo series based on notes that artists write to themselves. I half nodded and half ran my hand down the back of the settee, sweeping for the grinder.

I just thought we have so many artist friends right? So why not use them for something. Whenever I'm round their studios I love to read the sticky notes, or the posters, or the graffiti they leave, always urging their future creative selves to do something different or to try harder. They criticise their present to save their future. I think it's very introspective.
I think so too, as I sprinkle what she hasn't already smoked into the long paper.
Sometimes it's something stupid, like, RED IS THE NEW BLUE. Sometimes they're utterly indecipherable, a code that only they can crack in the heat of creative abandon. A lot of the time they're warnings. I got the idea at Kottie's the other night, he's into it. I think they can really offer insight into how

different artists work.
I think that's brilliant babe, as I lick the sticky paper. Who else have you got lined up?
Diego is in too. He has a sign that just says OPEN THE ENVELOPE. So I asked him what's in the envelope? He said he doesn't know, he can't remember what he wrote inside. He just remembers sealing the envelope and writing the instruction on the wall. So I said why don't you look? And he says he's saving it for when he really needs it. And Bella's in too. She made a huge poster for herself that just says GROW A PAIR.

I was genuinely impressed I thought as I lit my cone. Then I got an idea of my own.

You could use my notes if you like, I said, nodding at my desk littered with yellow squares of paper, a sprawl of tortured plans to action.

Her response floored me. Just when I thought the evening might have been going well, like we were getting along. Like she might have forgotten about my foiled wank.

Don't be silly. You're not an artist babe, you work in a call centre.

She whipped the joint from my fingers and put on her shoes and jacket. She blew a kiss to herself in the mirror and she walked out into the evening.

Nothing inside of me wanted to chase her, and play prey to her victim. The TV mumbled incoherently like a drunk in the corner, and the couch began to engulf me. The weight of my whale had begun to fall down upon my eyes. I got chance to glimpse longingly at my desk, and my notes decorating it like hieroglyphics. I could write in the morning I thought, before work, in my greys and in my blacks. And sleep eventually took it's welcoming hold.

From what I could now see was the very far side of the cavernous chamber, a pink flare shot diagonally through the air, shot from the gun of a silhouetted figure, standing in what can only be described as a boat. A black tunnel was visible in the short distance behind, a portal to the next stage of digestion. The flare trailed like a falling star, bringing a red glow to blitz the darkness of the whales belly, if only for a few seconds. But in those few seconds, I managed to glimpse my doom. Firstly, I was struck by the utter size of the place I found myself, dwarfingly high and long, like an industrial warehouse for fairytale giants. The flair revealed a roof of ribs as it skied upwards, levelling out beneath the curved ivory structures, scaffolding pink inner flesh. Then as it began to droop downwards, aimed somewhere near to where I stood, I gazed upon an indeterminable sea of feathers and beaks and necks and fluttering wings and beady black eyes. And as the flare floated into the ground, and it's red glow with it, I saw the geese, hundreds of them, for as far as the dying light could reveal, but their concentration hinted there could of been many hundreds more in the darkness. I felt more pecking at my ankles, but this time saw the culprits at my feet, just before the light of the flare died forever. The Dark Side was my only friend in this darkness.

I knew I had to get to that boat, and that now flareless man, and leave this land of Geese. I readied myself in the direction of my destination, more pecks and angry nibbles rushing me on. I stumbled forth into the mega-gander, the enraged hisses and pecks following me, and growing with every wet step. I splashed onwards, slow and steady at first, but with increased haste as the hisses grew and grew to a great cacophony of fury and outrage, and the biting beaks snapped at my legs, cutting and bruising, spurring me on. I was sprinting now, puddles and feathers splashing up behind me, with not much farther to go by my reckoning. I ploughed through the geese, sometimes stepping on a bird skull or broad white back so they could not hinder my progress, or strike my troubled legs. I began to feel the water I was running through growing deeper around my feet, slowly at first, but then quite sharply to just over knee high. I took that as a good sign that I must be fast approaching the boat, but with the downside of slowing me from a sprint to a muddy scuttle, each step more sticky than the last. The gradient did not cease, and neither did the geese, which were now no longer on their webbed feet but floating atop the water, able to peck at hips and ribs and kidneys, and so they did. I punched them away as best I could, but for every goose I hooked, two more beaks would strike from the darkness, catching a wrist or finger. I paddled forth with all my strength, but now the water was beyond my waist and I had to make the decision to cease wading and start swimming. I dived forward into the blackness, and began to stroke forward as fast as I could, but the geese were now pecking at my skull, snapping at my ears. And as I tried to palm my assailants away, one caught me square in the eye, the pain shooting to the back of my head like a rusty nail thrust through the retina. The sudden shock of pain caused me to search for the floor with my feet, but I did not find it in reach, causing me to take an unwelcome gulp of the salty whale stomach drink, as sharp beak after sharp beak sprang forth from the black, thudding against my skull and face, coiling and recoiling with deafening hisses. I was treading water as best I could, but my pain, blindness and aquatic discombobulation meant I now no longer knew which way lay the shallows, or which way the boat. I tried again to scream, but only took another mouthful of the disgusting water, spitting it out as yet another furious beak struck hard to my temple. I was being overcome, by the depth beneath me, the geese around me and the pain inside me. I was now drowning, but still I could not scream. Through the incessant chorus of hissing and splashing, and the water in my lacerated ears, I could hear a piano playing softly. I began to forget about my inflictions, the stinging wounds from my head to my toes, as the piano was joined by bass and guitar, the ethereal trio accompanying me to my beautiful death. I thought I was no longer frightened of dying. Why should he be afraid to die? My head went under, finally submerged. And the geese fell silent.

The digital screech of my alarm clock seemed to overlap the dead silence of the dream. I was almost pleased to see it was my first alarm, the red flashing fingers aligning in a 05:00 constellation. I had two hours to breathe life into my story, two hours to forget about the whale and the geese and Floyd.

As I stumbled over to my desk I noticed she was nowhere to be seen.

```
There wasn't a lot of ritual in our
rituals, but that was the point. I can't
```

remember how the drums started but they seemed fitting enough to say goodbye. Some of the elders confirmed that she was indeed dead, and they placed a crown of wild flowers upon her head. I watched them looking over the sad body, waiting to see if they too saw any evidence of murder. I wanted to run over and point them out to their untrained eyes, I wanted to check her vagina and under her nails and her legs and feet too, but nothing like this had happened in the Pile before and something, maybe Damo's stern words, stopped me when I should have taken action. It kept me unsure and kept me frozen as I saw the bodies worth of evidence prepared for cremation. The truth would have to be sought in secret. Some words were said to those who wanted to listen, a personal tribute rather than protocol, and she was thrust up once again and carried to the bonfire and lowered into the growing blaze. She wasn't our first to have flown and she wouldn't be our last.

I found Martha near the back of the crowd, many arms comforting her. She looked like the flames had made her see reason and her hysteria had left her. I asked her if we could speak alone and she nodded but didn't stray too far from those comforting arms.
'Martha my sister, I need to speak to

you.'
'I guess you want to talk about what happened down there at the lake?'
'Yes Martha, how do you think our sister died down there so early this morning?'
'I don't . . . I don't know. She must have drowned. I know she liked to go swimming early in the morning, to wake herself up. Oh I can't . . . I can't believe she's gone.'
She began to sniff the sour air as the tears came rolling back. I found myself studying them, looking for signs of sincerity. It was a long long time since I'd felt the innate electricity of suspicion.

I found Phillip in a similar position, but on the opposite curve of the circle. His arms were crossed and he was glazed over, staring somewhere deep into the white of the flames, beyond the heat and the body and the wood.
'Phillip my brother, I need to talk with you.'
His response came almost too quickly. He kept his eyes on the pyre and said that she had drowned.
'She must have drowned.'
He also knew how she loved a dip before breakfast, an apparently common knowledge I was not privy to previously. I saw hot red flags in the lick of the flames.

Damo was near the front now, on his knees with the others, urging our sister upwards. His head was bowed and he had pulled his great fur over his head like a hood. He rocked back and forth with his siblings, his knees in the dirt and his eyes closed tight. I tried to glimpse his face as he rocked backwards and raised his head with the great wave of the drums.

I asked myself if I really had seen a smile there on those hidden lips, just a momentary grin warped from evil? I could ignore the scratching inside no more, and I told myself that I had work to do, with Damo as my partner once again or not, it did not matter. I had work to do.

COLLEAGUES

People talk about the disconnect of the phone, how the lack of face to face, the eviction of eye contact and gesture, and most importantly (I thought) the removal of immediate physical violence, make it easier for people to disconnect themselves from what they're saying down those lines of wire and air. I couldn't disconnect myself from being called a cunt though, especially so often, no matter how often I resorted to my rituals, my ways out. I banned myself from looking at clocks, I distracted myself with hangovers and getting high in my half hour. I told myself it wasn't so serious, that it was all just a means to an end, and an end was always in sight. I'll finish that book soon, and then everything will be different for me, for us.

The biggest offender was not one of those many poor bastards I harassed for a pitiful living. It was in fact my team manager, a pastiche of a man if ever I've seen one. Or boss as he preferred to be addressed, even though I'm pretty sure he wasn't. He took a special liking to me, that's for sure. He had one of those faces. I can't give a meticulous Mannesque break down of said face, sometimes people just look like people. Sometimes people look like movie stars and sometimes people look like they should be in movies, we all spend an alternative life as casting agents, forever judging. But this guy just had one of those faces, metaphorically caved in from years of being punched in the minds of others.

I wasn't experiencing very much joy in my life at that time, but at least I knew it as an emotion I could sometime someday someplace know and respect and feel and absorb and reciprocate. He knew that was our fundamental difference, he knew he would never know, or knew that he couldn't know what it was I knew. And he held that against me with egregious prejudice, offering only a natural defensive state, a YOU THINK YOUR BETTER THAN ME sneer, a siege on his own mind which drove him retarded.

And naturally he got paid more than me.

Ows the buk coming along yer cunt? was one of his perpetual refrains. Why did I ever tell him (or anybody) about writing. Maybe I wanted to show him I was different, or to show myself that I didn't belong there. Either way, he took it as a lofty insult, which I guess was true too.

Ow did YOU get HER? was another, Yer lucky cunt as a stale full stop.

Yes he loved HER, or the thought of her at least. We'd bumped into him for one second of one minute of one evening, in town. I remember I couldn't shake his amateur hug and he took her hand and he kissed it. I could almost see the line of slime he left, still hanging between his crunchy lips and the hand it left there, languished by transgression.

I was never stuck in a race or a chase, there was a conspicuous lack of that kind of urgency. I was just that cunt who'd ring you as you sat down for dinner. Are you happy with your contract service provider service sir madam? You let me know that I'm the cunt that I am and hang up, and you go back to your lasagne and I go onto the next one. I wasn't always a cunt. Sometimes I'll catch a lonely old sir madam of the household and I could chat away to them and pretend I was real until they started repeating themselves, their minds and their mouths going round in circles. I knew how it felt, knowing something's not right but not knowing what's wrong.

I wasn't always a cunt.

Six years is a long time to be somewhere you never planned to be. I knew from day one that my new colleagues were total wankers. Hands-free wankers, I used to call them. I tried to hate them, their tea towel checked shirts, the smell of their hairgel and their hangovers, their hard sells and their high fives. But my hate was slowly tamed by the trappings of what constitutes reality, smiling back for the sake of my traineeship.

There was a cleaner there then called Kazim, a cupboard of a man who flanneled his way round with a curious industry. He would be on our floor for the first couple of hours of play, fiddling quietly in the background.

In some misguided attempt to distance myself from my colleagues I decided to try and buddy up with the cleaner, offering him a morning coffee or a soup powder from a sachet. We'd chat about our different paths, our different ghosts, his old country and my imagined one. We'd share looks of indifference towards the slime balls around us. I did my best to assure him I wasn't one of them, that I was but a temporary spectator to this partitioned world. Kazim accepted me as an equal, a friend and to his downfall, his confidante.

It started when he told me he'd been pilfering from the building for years undetected, which I honestly regarded as perfectly acceptable and legitimate. But one day, when I was nearing the end of my traineeship, I was summoned by the almighty one to his office, who as it happens didn't share my Robin Hood reasoning. The aforementioned team leader, the aspirant bully who chained my gang sat just behind him, his chin pointing to a grin, his nothing arse perched on the desk flank.

He informed me straight off that my entire traineeship hung in the balance. He listed the various office equipment that had recently been noted to be missing and presumed stolen. The list was long and eclectic, from stationary to scanners and screens, all nabbed when nobody was looking. Sheriff John had a prime suspect though, and he needed me to play the grass and give up my buddy Kazim. I shocked myself by how quickly I flipped. I hid in the toilet playing snake as they escorted him off the premises.

The drums had long died down and the crowd slowly dispersed as the fire crackled away. They had said their goodbyes and went back to the daily tasks which occupied us all. I tried to study their faces as they quietly left the circle, looking for a story to follow.

I saw Martha and Phillip were stood together once again, and I noticed they were both looking at me. They stopped looking as I returned their dual gaze, and both stared again at the charred remains. I needed to talk to them, I needed to get my detective duty back in order but it had been so many long years I had got it all wrong so far.

Suspicion, crime, corruption, Murder; words we had long lost at the Pile. I tried to think as my old self would have thought, and for the first time since I left that world I regretted forgetting it. Phillip whispered something in Martha's ear and they turned from the circle and walked slowly off together into the humble jumble sanctuary of the Pile. I lifted my fur up over my head like a cowl and followed their footsteps cautiously.

A hand grabbed me on the shoulder not long into my covert pursuit. I span around to see another hooded figure like me, grasping my shoulder in earnest. It was Damo.
'Sorry for my grave words before brother' he said looking profoundly into my eyes. 'I was greatly troubled by what I saw.' His face was serious and fittingly grim.
'I understand brother. I was too, and still I am. But I can't let it be forgotten, the signs we saw. I know it's wrong to feel what I felt, letting my old self take hold. But this is something I cannot ignore.'
'I see that too, I really do' he concurred, 'I too felt those ghouls and that's why I was so eager to hand her over to the Pile. I saw in the flames how selfish that was of me. But you must understand, our people have long forgotten about these things brother. It would be dangerous to start throwing these ideas around before we have some truth in our hands, it would mean the return of many phantoms for many people. Phantoms they've spent years exorcising, shadows that would be perilous to the pure foundations of our community.'
'I understand. Our hunt for the truth will

stay undisclosed. But we will hunt all the same. Come, I feel Martha and Phillip could shed more light. I was hoping to talk more with them just now.'
'I agree. Maybe it's just that spectre we thought was spent. But I too feel like they have more to reveal.'

It had been a long time since I'd felt the base buzz of the hunt, and it came back so strongly that it felt innate. Me and my old partner back in pursuit, driven as we always were by truth and justice. But we'd left that orbit for a reason, leaving our stories behind, consigning them to the myth of others just so we could move on. Damo's story felt as much a part of my own, the story of what had finally sent us running from our jobs and lives and from the exhausting fever of progress. It was all coming back, thawing my tampered mind's eye, a scalding deliquesce.

Damo was a single parent. His son claimed to not remember his mother, but she died when he was two, the noxious legacy of a drunken driver. I remember it well when it returns, even though I worked and drank and sniffed my way through it all. And so did Damo. I became a part of his sons life, mainly by proxy, a distant faux uncle, but a part nonetheless. I was that guy in the pub who reminded him that he remembers when he was born, when he was this high, and so on and on, as he nods politely and grabs his wankered dad from the pub I'd been keeping him in all afternoon. Damo tried his best, but a cops free time is hallowed, and his kid often came second to the pursuit.

He never wanted to play football on the green in front of their flat with the other boys. He preferred to play on his own in the dusty living room after school, shunning those raucous boys and their unreflective affronts. He preferred to play indoors, grounding bonds of immortal friendship between his toys, building cities in the gaudy patterns of the carpet. But he was turning out alright, a victory for nature over nurture, growing up quick, sharp, wise and friendly all at the same time. Damo could count himself lucky for that. They say you can't choose your family. But sometimes you just get lucky.

School sped by like a train, en route into the unknown. It was actually my idea to get him the job, acting on his Dads worries regarding his child's enduring lonerdom. He was 13 years old. I knew a woman who owned a laundrette. She was vile and round, a bulldog chewing on electricity, intent on every character of cancer. But she needed someone on the weekend, and I hoped it would do the boy some good. Get him out of his shell. Work can make a talker out of us all, just like love.

There wasn't a lot we hadn't seen in those days, Damo and I. The cardinal blows of human cruelty, year upon year of variants on the most hideous of themes, murder and rape and abuse. Man on man, man on woman, man on child and every other alternative you could rouse in any revulsive nightmare.

A girl we found on Christmas day in a graveyard the year before. She should have finished me off.

I'd had a dramatic Christmas eve the night before and realised I was probably still drunk as I squelched my horn outside Damo's flat. He had to leave his son to his own devices, after a brief flurry of present opening and hugs early in the holiday morning.
'He'll be fine, he always is', and we headed to the graveyard, the bright yellow scene tape bouncing through the wet mist, the brown slush around the headstones and the long dead flowers. This was no white christmas.

She was 13, the same age as the boy. Her unborn had been cut out of her. Her mangled body had been kicked into the ashen bushes. It looked like he'd had another go too, before or after, we couldn't tell.

We chopped out lines in a grotty pub toilet, the tiles as yellow as pissy nicotine. It was the afternoon after, on boxing day. Sometimes we talked shop, chatted out our thoughts, sometimes even feelings. But the girl of the day before was not one of those. Hers was a mournful shake of the head, staring deep into the bottom of your pint, into oblivion. A 'the world is fucked' stare and ghastly silence.

But we did talk about something else, what Damo had come home to find later on his Christmas day. He confided in me there in the cubicle, as he always could. He told me when he got back from the station, a little earlier than he had forewarned, he found his son dressed in stockings and suspenders and a tiny tight dress. He had music on loud and didn't hear his Dad come in. He was dancing and miming in the flats only mirror.

It's then he saw his Dad over his shoulder in the reflection, and fell down onto his knees and cowered. Damo told me the boy wouldn't stop crying, and apologising through the tears. Damo told me he had thought about it for too long before he got down next the boy and calmed him down from his hysteria.
'I'm sorry dad, i'm sorry i'm sorry' he bawled. Damo didn't know what to say back.

After he'd become relatively placated they endeavoured to chat. Damo was a good father at heart, just not with heart, as that would have required him to be there more often. Damo was confused as to where the clothes had come from, there were no women in their life in that flat. His son explained that he'd be stealing them from the laundrette. Damo couldn't even bring himself to admonish the boy for the theft, so vulnerable the boy looked, his amateur mascara weeped down his cheeks, his breathing stressed and snotty.

The pig faced woman at the laundrette soon started receiving complaints. Bras and french knickers missing, dresses not where they should be. Someone must have been through my clothes when I had my head in a book or when I popped outside for a fag, that kind of thing. She looks back at the

camera the boy didn't know she had. And
caught him red handed.

She grabbed him by the ear and marched him
out into the busy saturday street.
'GET THE FUCK OUT OF MY SHOP YOU THIEVING
LITTLE QUEER' she screamed as she thwacked
him over the back of the head. She wanted
to make the biggest loudest scene she
could.
'I DON'T WANT TO SEE YOUR FACE AGAIN YOU
SICK PERV, GO ON FUCK OFF.'
All the eyes and ears of the high street
now focused in on the spectacle of shame.
'GET TO FUCK YOU DIRTY LITTLE BASTARD. HEY
EVERYBODY, THAT KID ROBS LADIES UNDERWEAR,
THAT LITTLE GAYBOY THERE YEAH THAT'S HIM.
NASTY QUEER' her words chased him up the
street.

Some people tutted, some people laughed. A
gang of five of who had witnessed it
decided to follow the boy. They were all
his age or above. They carried on the
verbal torture as he broke out into a run.
'WHERE YOU RUNNING TO FAGGOT. GOT SOME
DICKS TO SUCK.'

His running away only made it worse.
Nothing inspires a ring of bored teenagers
into a tribal chase then a victim on the
run. They soon had the boy cornered,

trapped down an alley like a pathetic animal.

They probably didn't mean to kill him. But words soon turned to fists, as soon as the big boy put one in then the others felt the compulsion to join in, deranged by the crowd. They put the boot in too, and that's what finished him. A kick to the wrong part of his skull and he was gone forever.

It had been many years now since I'd thought about that time, so determined I had been to forget it. It looked like there was no stopping it now. I wondered if Damo was thinking about it too as we followed Martha and Phillip silently down to the lake, like two ancient hunters in the wake of their quarry. Using the stealth of distance straight back to the scene of the crime. The crisp shore from where our sister had flown.

ESCAPE

Two strong arms pulled me up from the blackness, an island scene in that sea of Geese. I was numb, blind and full of water, but I felt those two arms plunge in above me and take me by the scruff of my neck. Like a toddler gone limp to the overwhelming power of an adult, I was grabbed under my armpits, and dragged aboard the vessel. Life shot through me as soon as I felt the wooden floor of the life boat on my back, and I rolled onto my side to expel what was drowning me. I coughed and spluttered, but when I searched for a 'Who are you?' or a 'Where am I?' it did not come. I lifted myself by my renewed elbows to a sit. The water began to leave my ears, and I heard that piano again. I thought it to be so beautiful that maybe I had drowned. And then a fantastic voice, a woman's voice, bellowed out from the ether. This most angelic scream encircled the boat and my mind, and I thought surely I had now passed. In front of my face, the figure, my saviour, stirred above. A match was struck and a lamp was lit. The angels voice ploughed on, up and down, from beautiful chaos to restless warble. My saviour moved the now glowing lamp to his face, revealing himself. It was Damo.

The same Damo from my story had infiltrated my powerful dream. I recognised his face from how I had painted it, a face that only exists in the imaginations of others, each painting him as they see fit. But gone were the natural fibres I had given him, and on his head lay steady a black wide rimmed hat, decorated by a shiny black bow, sombrely tied. The rim was wide enough to cover his eyes when tilted forward, as was now. He wore a Gestapoesque black leather trench coat over his thin shoulders.

And in his mouth rested a most magnificent spliff, a joint of Arthurian legend, shrouded in medieval glamour and old world authority, piercing like a jousters tool to the lungs. It was fittingly dreamy in its awe and girth. It was like a dunces cap without the D, brimming with green trees that glowed like kryptonite. He used the lamp to light his herb and took an almighty drag. He straightened his spine and then, summoning some insipid magic, he stretched his mouth, in the most ungodly fashion, to the size of a chimney perched atop a steam train. His jaw seemed elastic or liquid and his chimney gob manifested there with its elongated circumference. Then as if the train was racing, he blew the smoke in a slow thick cloud down upon my face. I felt the dense cloud engulf my sodden body and clothes. I coughed and spluttered like a Yugoslavian auto. I was blind again, but I did not see black, only white.

My elbows fell from beneath me and I fell back onto the wood. Like a felled tree I clunked against the floor. A crazed smile broke out on my face, as my hands slapped myself hard on the cheeks, as if to awaken myself, or to check I was already awake. It was futile of course.

Damo had already taken the oars, and began to row, the lamp lighting the tunnel they were headed for, leaving the land of Geese forever. I giggled at a now distant last hiss, as I stared into my heavenly white cloud, and The Great Gig in the Sky.

```
I looked at Damo and noticed a wetness to
his eyes, maybe he really had been
thinking of his son again, a forbidden
memory we had quietly shared as events
unfolded. It somehow felt that these
events, this day, had been coming.

I realised then that I hadn't even asked
Damo why he was down at the lake this
morning. Who had found Kyra's body? Why
were any of them there in fact? I knew I
should have been asking these questions,
but our proximity to our suspects required
```

silence and I knew I'd have to wait for Damo's answers.

The deceleration of my life at the Pile had occluded my instincts for this old game. Patience is often a virtue, but I knew swift guile was recurrently righteous, but where had mine gone? I hadn't even asked myself these questions. Why had I woken up on that rock and not my usual cot back at the Pile? How thick was that fog this morning? What was I even doing last night? I struggled to tally my memory, and whose service it was in. Regardless, it seemed like good sense to follow Martha and Phillip.

The lake shone in the distance like the silver coins we had long since deserted. Martha and Phillip traipsed ahead of us moodily, and we ducked and covered our way behind them.

It seemed fitting that they were my least favourite siblings at the Pile. They felt like a team to me, a team I was never picked for. I loved all my brothers and sisters unconditionally but Martha and Phillip had always kept me at a cruel distance. In the thin posterior of my brain I knew it was because I used to be police. They never let it be known, in an explicit sense, in speech or looks or action, but I knew. It was intrinsic and suppressed, a prejudice they had buried rather than burnt. But I knew, and so did Damo. He too had felt their silent disdain.

The lake blushed with radiant reflection and I had to shield my eyes, our distrustees painted silhouettes. Their own stories began to seep into my consciousness as I studied their outlines under the buttress of my palm. Both of their stories had been revealed to me over the years, through gossip of course, but mainly through our group chats, or therapy as they would've called it in the old new world. We called it Journeying, and our collectiveness required us to Journey every day, where we made revelations and de-cloaked, how we let go of our tragedies and moved on.

I remembered hearing of how Martha had lived, before. Staying under whatever roof wouldn't kill her, on the floors of harsh cells, or in the fire escapes of various crumbling modern monstrosities. She was a big girl in a small gang, and they made their money on the street. She wasn't a prostitute, but those poor girls were her biggest victims. Particularly those Eastern European girls with that shiny long natural hair. They hit at night, and were swift and brutal.

Martha had been up to it for years before the carnage caught up with her. The CCTV footage was the proof that she was the leader of the pack, the one who would strike the first blow, and the one with the razor. The other girls would pin their victim to the tarmac after Martha had flown in first with fist and foot. They'd hold their mark on the cold damp pavement and Martha would go to work on their hair, taking the razor and removing a full head of it.

She was more of a surgeon then a barber, working with vicious precision and brute speed. She didn't mind if she took a chunk of scalp off too though, as long as she got those long locks; straight or curly, black, brown, blonde or red. They'd bag them up and leave the poor girl lying there, shawn and senseless. They'd sell the natural hair to the merchants who'd make them into extensions and wigs for the vain and the insecure. It was good money, for a time.

When she got out of prison she walked out of those gates and just kept on walking. Walking from the city to the towns and through the villages, and then to the mountains and beyond, to the Pile. She was re-born after that odyssey, and her Journey continued with us all. She claimed to be a new person, but how could I be so sure? I was finding out that even after all my Journeys, I hadn't changed so much. I was slowly slipping back into my old roles, the hunter, the detective, an authority. Maybe not as quickly as I now wished I could, but it was certainly cooking, and an old dawn was rising.

The fog of that morning still sat stagnant inside my head, my memory searching through it like the hopeful beams of a lighthouse. I felt like I knew my old self better than what I was now, what I had become. And I felt resentful. Resentful for what this place had made me, rendering me what I now saw as ineffective, unable to ask the most basic of questions, impotent in the face of such a callous crime. A murderer was out there and I couldn't keep up, and the fog grew thicker.

I learnt Phillip's story too over the years, and I had always harboured my suspicions about his claims to sanity. He was a myrmecologist, a budding sociobiologist, who would travel from woodland to meadow to garden to highland to lowland in search of his beloved ants. Ants and their colonies, their great cities built on collective will. He was enamoured by the super-organism, dedicating his life to cracking the codes of the ants, the ancient secrets to their success.

Funding came and went and suitable positions were hard to come by. Books were started, and abandoned. Theories circled like vultures before disappearing over the horizon. But still the ants nested and thatched and fertilised and worked and worked and worked. He was struggling to maintain relationships with his own species, spending more and more time with his venerable insects.

He would look down upon their megalopolises, the guts hidden beneath bark or soil or sand, and ask them politely to reveal themselves. He spent the last of his inheritance on trips along the Mediterranean, the coast of California and the west coast of Japan, witnessing the vast super-colonies of the tiny Argentine ant, all linked by genes, all one great big global family.

It was when he returned from this trip, utterly broke, and with nothing to show but a crippling wonderment, an awe for this global mega-colony which inspired nothing but piety, that he lost his house and went to live in the forest. He justified it as a last resort, a shot at deep practise and enlightenment to his cause, but it was clearly the onset of madness. He hoped the ants would take him away, thousands of them carrying him down into their perfect world, but all he got were stings and bites. He stopped asking them politely and would shout down upon their worlds, kicking their soil roofs into oblivion, and then watching them through teary apologetic eyes deal with that destruction, time and time again.

One day he came across a field on the forest boundary, and there he saw a hot air balloon awaiting lift off. He watched it from the sanctum of the bramble, the envelope filling to it's full and eager potential. He was reminded of his time in Borneo with the leaf cutter ants, he'd flown a hot air balloon there and seen the limitless beauty of the tropical canopy, gliding above like a silent bird. How happy he was to see that place, and then return to the ground and see the skilled ants in action. He chose to seize the moment.

He ran out from his forest, stinking and dishevelled, and screaming. There were two balloonists ready for take off, but when they saw Phillip running wildly towards them, they chose to abandon the basket to the half beast. He commandeered the floating vessel and headed preposterously upward into the quiet sky, the silence only broken by generous blasts of the burner, and the fading voices from the ground begging him to come back down.

But that was the last thing on his mind.

The wind was thirsty and bold and took him back over his forest, where he thought of the ants underneath, oblivious to his plight, unimpressed by his flight.

Soon he came to the town he had previously forsaken, and had to rise again to avoid the power lines. It was an old market town of decent size and the tight streets hustled and bustled with the charge of rush hour. Phillip observed from his soaring plinth, seeing his old house in the high street and wondering who now slept in his bed and bathed in his bath.

He saw the terrain for what it was; houses, streets, shops, roads, cars, bins, train tracks, parks, and factories. He saw the little dots darting back and forth, in and out, round and round. He saw the little dots bypass each other seamlessly, sometimes stopping to relay information to one another, or just moving by like fluid. He saw the little dots engage in exchange like some material trophallaxis.

He saw the little dots nest and thatch and fertilise and work and work and work. He was the observer once again, detached from his subjects, detached from the ground, and in the turmoil of detaching from himself. He thought about the little dots down below, all following their talents, all good for something, all contributing to a collective something. All individuals. But what was he good for? What was his talent? These are the questions he asked himself as he cowered down into the basket, feeling the pull of the onward wind, as he longed for his ants. His talented ants, defined by craft, unified by progress, all aware of their genius, all aware of their individuality. He closed his eyes tight and awaited the crash.

When he got out of hospital he walked out of those gates and just kept on walking. Walking from the city to the towns and through the villages, and then to the mountains and beyond, to the Pile.

The black and red box appeared for it's daily warning, as it had done every day for the past thirteen months. Your virus protection software has expired, please update immediately. The drop down menu revealed the escape route of choice and habit, Remind me in one day, a motto I found impelled to adopt. Remind me in one day, if only every job, every relationship, every social interaction, every message, every bill had that same drop down menu option. I tried my best to implement my own Remind me in one day manifesto but the ringing in my ears, that banshee scream of what purports to be real, it's too piercing to ignore. If reality was dead it had one hell of a ghost.

I remembered Damo and his role in my dream. It felt like the onset of madness. A character I had plucked from my subconscious was now ruling it. The stench of trouble filled my cavities, like a hot turd in the sun, trapped between inescapable wafts of anxiety. It felt like Damo was in my stomach too, rowing his boat, playing his record, splashing around and bouncing off the walls.

I got too drunk at the dinner party. Her friends as usual. She still maintains the fallacy that I'm a writer to them, she's never divulged the reality of my day to day to that group, none of whom had ever set foot in a call centre. The wine had found a way to flow towards me, like a noria perpetually scooping up the liquid, and watering the fields. I grew in my hatred towards their lovely hands and their rubbish conversation and their useless regurgitation of something resembling opinion. My god-given right to interrupt grew loudly with every glass, every hydro spin of the water wheel, and she stared at me across the table like we were over.

If only one of us had the strength.

One of them asked me how to make it good as a writer, what it was like to be an artist. I looked across at her, her eyes still drilling into me, searching for the other side. She inspired me into a tirade of sarcasm that the wine in me was delighted to hear.

I told them that you need to do whatever it takes to achieve your dreams. I told them it's a world of competition, but this competition has no rules, no referees. There's no such thing as friends too in this competition, only other competitors, so be sure to be sceptical of collaboration. And if you do take the collaborative route make sure to come out the beneficiary, bullish stubbornness is a key strength here. I told them that to borrow ideas can make you look weak, but to steal ideas makes you look original, and I learnt that from Picasso so it must be right.

They nodded like I was a fucking oracle, making approving mumbles and sipping away. I was delighted that they didn't get it, so I carried on. Her eyes still pierced but my vino armour was thick.

I told them it's important not to isolate your audience, so avoid anything too "clever" (I used my fingers for the ersatz marks). The trick is to appear different, but fundamentally be the same, it's a fine line to tread but the spoils are worthwhile. Always trust the judgement of those who have made it before you, they must know what they're talking about if they've achieved what you haven't. It's always a good idea to appease these kinds of people above you on the ladder. At the same time, never relinquish anything to the people who are below you on the ladder, its a real sign of weakness. It's actually a better idea to manipulate these kinds of people to your advantage, they'll do anything for a shot at what you've got. I told them that the trick is to leave the door open enough for them to see through, but never enough to pass through, and they all seemed to like the analogy, scribbling it down furiously in their minds. I think I even saw one of the wretches make a note of it in her diary, maybe even sketching a tiny door slightly ajar.

But the most important thing I told them was to always, no matter what, just be yourself. But none of them seemed to write that part down.

OWNERSHIP

You're earning money now love you should be buying a house, preached my old lady. Come on son, it's about time you got yourself on the property ladder. You've got yourself a steady job now preached my old man. Buy a house they relentlessly advised over and over for the best part of a year. Buy a house, it's the best investment you can make, buy a house, you wont regret it.

So I went to the bank with my dad, and I went to the agents with my mum, and I got my two bedroom flat by the river.

Oh isn't it lovely dear fawned ma as we thumbed the sticky menus of the chain pub plonked next to our new builds. I ordered the gammon and chips and about a year later I'd lost about fifty grand on the shoddy box.

That was our home now, where we lived together.
It just needs a woman's touch she said when she decided she

was moving in. I took that to mean more pillows and candles and I don't think I was wrong.

I would have preferred to move into hers, but that apparently was never on the table. I loved her falling down house in that other part of town, not by the river. Its decrepitude, its constant state of decline. The hole in the stairs you had to evade in the morning, the drum kit in what used to be a hall. The holes in the walls where birds now lived and shat down the walls. Mine was the opposite, a flimsy bastille of platitude. A vapid cubicle. With added pillows.

The greys and blacks of those winter mornings dissipated into the greys of spring, and at some point, the greys and blues of summer. I didn't notice, I hadn't got up early early for months.

The story I was writing was blocked, physiologically speaking. Mainly because I was filling my evenings with overtime, on all of my six days if I could. I had to keep it all together, and my book would have to wait. I guess it wasn't going anywhere anyway. Every obvious canal in my brain ached, and every feasible muscle reciprocated. Those two hours I somehow wrought to write were lost to selling more crap on the phones, and feeble shallow sleep.

She couldn't find any work, like the rest of the city it seemed. On my one day off we'd sometimes see friends. We'd get together in those bars that weren't pubs and they'd tell me how they were holding onto work with their fingertips, or slipping between improbable interviews, 'we've had over three thousand applicants for this position, why should we give it to you?' kind of thing.

I completely understood. There were rumours going through my offices of scaling back, streamlining, consolidating, even rationalising. I was terrified into performance, smashing 'my' targets with coerced surety. My ship was certainly sinking, but thankfully slower then everyone else's. I dreaded to think what would happen if I couldn't pay my mortgage and my water and my gas and my electricity and my car insurance and my council tax and my phone and my internet and my tv license and my petrol and my national insurance and my overdraft charges and my gym and my credit card and my road tax and my sky. I would have loved to even pretend that I didn't care about that dystopia, but a panic still choked me every time I imagined that shit storm. And it was the panic which kept me going, an angst in my stomach which released not just butterflies, but giant hairy moths, brown and crazed and bouncing off every digestive wall. I could only fend them off by keeping my head, or our heads, above the rising water. Surely we wouldn't have to tread here forever.

We're really getting the best of this global warming she comments as the summer imposes itself like an unshakeable stink. The heat cemented itself to everything and everyone, mired to a people not used to it. I sweated in my short sleeve shirts, avoiding the beauty of the sky outside the office windows, so tempting in it's halcyon hue, a visible heaven asking us to fuck it all off.

If only.

We had a very fat Nigerian family next door, our lives separated by the so called walls. There was a fat Grandma, a fat Mother, a fat Father, a very fat man I was never introduced to, and three fat children. They would waddle around the flat shouting at each other. The shouting only seemed to cease when it would, without warning, break into an eruption of wonderful laughter. Laughter so rich, so deep and honest that when I heard it I felt everything might just turn out OK.

The children were forever chewing or peeling or sucking on some edible grasped in their chubby hands. In their own way, despite being the smallest, they were the fattest of the whole family. They were so fat I wondered whether I should of being informing social services, surely it was some form of child cruelty, just as bad as starving a child. I figured out that the difference was love, to feed is to love, and there was a lot of love in that house.

I would look at her skinny starving frame as she slipped into her gym clothes in the bathroom, every bone jutted out but still she looked at them with disgust. She didn't know I was looking and she would slam the door shut when she caught me. I wondered how much love was in our house.

When I was a child I thought adults were all invincible. Then in high school our physics teacher hung himself. He said in his note that he could not take us anymore, he even specifically named my class. He'd seen all that was unfixable in the world in our puberty ravaged faces, and said he had to do it to himself before he did it to us. He mentioned no specific names, but I guess I had crossed the line with him, pushed him in my own way to the brink. I once slotted a tub of cod liver oil capsules individually through the gaps of the radiator in his office. They melted slowly, unleashing a cruel stench. I never owned up, but others did worse, much much worse. I thought of him as I saw my wobbly self again, reflected on the side of the bus that had come to take me to hell once more. This was my wobbly life as an invincible adult.

If I was lucky enough to get a seat on the bus or the train, and could keep my head from nodding capriciously between stops, I'd get my pen and paper out. This was my time to write now, hiding my slow sentences from the nosey commuters hemmed in all around me.

Martha and Phillip hung by the edges of the lake like sorry reeds. Damo and I dangled back in observation, peeking out from behind a craggy edge. The fog of that sorrowful morning had long burnt away and the two hooded figures stood seemingly silent looking out to the lake and its secrets. They could have been whispering but we could not tell from the distance we had kept, looking down the slope and waiting for them to make their move.

The fog before our eyes may have vanished, but behind my eyes a fog still wallowed. Being so close to the lake again only served to thicken it, as if it was somehow congealing, curdling my thoughts and memories. I took my eyes away from our targets for a few seconds, to rub my face with my palms and my eyes with my fingers. I caught Damo looking at me without pity. I must remember to ask him those questions. I must remember.

Martha and Phillip made their move, and their actions only sufficed to further arouse my suspicions. They both began to disrobe, dropping their cloaks and hides to the ground, layer by layer until nude. They peeled off their boots and stepped gingerly into the lake. They strode out and dipped under, letting the cold water purge their clumpy hair and naked bodies. 'A strange time for a swim' I muttered to my partner.
'Indeed' he grunted, not taking his eyes off the couple.
The naked figures embraced each other waist high in the lake. It soon became clear however that this was no hug of condolement. Their tongues explored each others mouths and necks. Their hands glided between fronts and backs and sides. They were exercising their rights as neighbours.

We were all brothers and sisters at the Pile, and we were all neighbours too. Or lovers as they used to say in the civilised condition, as if the most complex emotion of the human being was so one dimensional. We were all neighbours and nobody belonged to anybody else.

Monogamy was an ill advised course as far as we were concerned, a civil trap, a fad and a dinosaur both. When we neighboured there were no assumed arrangements, no lies or exhortation. Just the implicit freedom of choice and all the pleasure it derived. Pleasures of the flesh, and pleasures of a free being too. There was and never would be ownership at the Pile, of spaces and things, and of minds and genitals.

Martha now had her back to Phillips front, her knees and hips at an angle allowing him entry. He ploughed away, every jolt forward causing her to squirm, as if on her last legs. She grabbed back at his chest with her thin fingers, but couldn't quite reach. His lower teeth gripped his bottom lip hard, twisting his face into a grimace. He dug away, clutching her pointy hips and her superfluous escape. We could hear them now from our hiding spot, nothing lucid save the gasps and exhalations of animal emotion, ancient and simple.

The flesh and its sounds of contact complete with the lusty splash of the lake began to stir me. I grew under the rough insides of my trousers and felt the pleasure of that gruffness on my cock. I tried to remember the last time it had been that hard.

Damo coughed awkwardly next to me, maybe feeling the chaos of my thoughts. He too was staring at the scene, but he did not run his tongue over his lips like I did. My cock began to ache so I fetched it from under my cloak and held it tight in my hand to stop it dancing. Damo saw what I was doing and so looked back at the show, out of discomfort or disgust I did not know. Or care, for the unstoppable tide had turned over me, I was engrossed, and now my hand was moving. Phillip and Martha worked away in the distance, unaware of the voyeurs sat behind the rock, one lost in some vacant stew, the other wanking uncontrollably.

'You should go join in brother' wheezed Damo into my ear 'They wont mind, we're all neighbours here remember.'
'Really brother? You think so?' I snorted back, unable to stop my hand greasing away, my head wobbling childishly, my face in a horny sulk.
'Yes brother, go join. You look like you need it' he said, alluding to my worked cock with his nod. I was now rubbing it against the cold hard rock.
'Maybe I will, maybe I will' I concluded, resuming my eyes on the fuck fest.

I had gotten quite close before they saw me. I'd broken cover and strolled down to the shore, tossing myself off menacingly as I walked. I expected my fellow

neighbours to greet me with dirty smiles
and welcoming tongues, but the mood
changed like a giant record needle had
scratched across the skies, abandoning us
in silence. It was far worse than a frigid
reception or an uncouth refusal. Far
worse.

'IT'S YOU!' they screamed in cold concert,
immediately quitting their sex and
sexuality.
'YOU! GET AWAY FROM US! WHAT DO YOU THINK
YOU'RE DOING HERE?' Martha wailed through
fresh tears.
'HOW DARE YOU! HOW COULD YOU!' cried
Phillip, now striding out towards me, his
falling fists, his dancing cock down by
his knees.
'GET AWAY FROM US GET AWAY FROM US!'
continued Martha, in nothing short of full
horror.

I went from the chaos of lust to an even
deeper turmoil, teeming with confusion and
rejection, wrenched like a planetary
collision. My cock fell away like ice
under the tap and I shrunk back. Phillip
continued his approach with an ever
violent gait. He strode through the water
like he dragged chains behind him, like
he'd broken from bondage through the sheer
power of rage. He was a gesture away from
thumping his chest, and his obscene
screams sent me scarpering. I used my head
start to flee. And as I passed the rock I

**had previously hidden behind I noticed
Damo no longer lay there in wait.**

She's reading Brave New World when I come in from work. It's good she says, have you read it? Very Orwellian she says. Like 1984 she says. I guess Orwellian rolls off the tongue better than Huxleyian, she says. It's good, have you read it? I've had enough of Eton boys, I mumbled back.

How did it go at the job centre I ask, envisioning miscarried crocodile tears at the emergency loans desk.
They wanted me to go to an interview at a bottling factory she huffed, can you imagine?
No. No I can't.

I pictured her signing on in huge sunglasses and an outfit that cost more than a months worth of benefits. She'll hold her handbag in her lap like it was a child prince, and saunter over cautiously, like she was scared of stepping in wet shit. And Ciao she'd say after the dole man gives her another weeks money for wine and garments.

She has started saying Ciao all the time now. It's only a matter of time before she's saying it for Hello as well. We're not in Europe I told her.
Yes we are, she snapped back.

In Europe, but not of it. It's funny how the little things grate the most.

I ate the roast chicken with my hands.
What are you, an animal? she hissed.
Yes. Yes I am.

When we got back from the restaurant she went online to review the restaurant. One star out of five she admonished, including a particularly cruel audit of the waitress. Maybe I'd spent too long admiring her tights and the button undone on her white blouse thing. She forced the analysis upon me, shepherding my face to the screen. It read like a list of first world problems, as did the rest of the site; the decor was vulgar, my children were victimised for playing by the coffee machine, the hand soap in the toilet was coarse, that kind of thing.

I've got a shoot tomorrow she said.
Wow. Good news, it's been a while I said, instantly regretting it.
OH FUCK YOU. TWAT she outraged, grabbing my can of lager and throwing it across the room. IT'S BEEN HARD OK, I'M TOO FUCKING OLD AND FAT IS THAT WHAT YOU WANT TO HEAR, DO YOU? I'M SORRY I'M TOO OLD AND FAT TO PAY RENT. THANKS A LOT, TWAT.
The door was slammed and she was out of it, storming off into the night, coat in hand. I felt jealous. She was the only one who could run away.

From the light of Damo's lamp, I lay on my back looking up at the tunnel roof passing above, our omnipotent soundtrack unwavering and amplified by the tightness of the tunnel. My bones ached from my ordeal in The Land of Geese but it was an ache of exhaustion, and the throbbing of my wounds had subsided thanks to Damo's exhaled medicine. I looked up at him now, locked into a steady row, the oars grafting a splashy propulsion, onwards through this long tunnel. Damo had still not uttered a word, and neither had I, but I certainly felt that his silence was more optional than mine. The tunnel roof no longer looked so red and fleshy, as it did at it's entrance where we had left the great stomach.

The roof had slowly darkened, the flesh rotting, turning to the ill brown of old meat, and increasingly to a dry dead black. In parts the decay was peeling away, hanging down like huge scabby flaps, and I heard a substantial chunk break free and splosh down into the water somewhere near our boat. I wondered how many other potential scab-bergs lay floating ahead, eager to pierce our vessel like crusty sirens. I wanted to sit up and keep a watch, but the weight of my limbs was pinning to me to the wooden floor of the boat, prone like a horizontal Christ. I could only stare upwards at the rotten roof and the music which bounced around us. The angels voice of heavenly soul had slowed and ceased now, and as the last fragments of piano and bass faded too, a monotonous crackle hung in the air, the sound of a needle looping round and round, trapped in its crackly rut.

The roof had now reached a full blackness, charred and ashen. Damo was unmoved, still silently rowing in his big black hat. It was then that we bore witness to some divine intervention. The incessant circular crackling was brought to an end by a loud piercing scratch which shook us and everything around us. It was the sound of a needle lifted impertinently from its berth, freed for the moment at least. It shook the roof above us so much that another scabby chandelier creaked loose and plummeted downwards. I waited for the splash which was surely too close for comfort, but it never came, and suddenly all was in mute. It was as if my ears had suddenly filled with treacle, I could hear nothing, and see nothing but the crumbling dead roof. Then just as abruptly as it had arrived, it left. The deafness was broken by another piercing scratch, unclogging my ears and filling the stale air with that crackle once again. I wondered which cruel and glorious God had flipped the record, setting the needle on its next winding journey?

I now began to see searching roots and branches weaving through the carbon ceiling, locking together and growing denser. The crackle was overtaken by cash registers chinging away again, opening and closing with the comforting groove of commerce. The roots and branches above steadily overcame the blackness, until the tunnel roof was now a thick blanket of tree limbs woven and fused together. I felt renewed as I saw this new living ceiling, and as the bass guitar joined the groove of commerce with driving synergy, I realised I could rise up within the little boat. First onto my rump, then to my knees, then slowly to my feet. Damo was still robotically ploughing through the drink, but seeing my new found erectness he at last acknowledged me with a sneer. My eyes were utterly captivated by what now faced Damos back, the very direction we were headed. My head swam with the sounds of Money, as I savoured upon the warmth of the light at the end of the tunnel.

UNREST

It was a long time since I'd seen a threat of violence at the Pile, let alone violence directed at me. It was another concept we had long abandoned, something that had no place here in our new world. Toil and struggle and loss will take their toll on any living soul, but in our community we refused violence as a solution to these woes. It's consequences always outweighed it's poor talent for resolution.

And of course we opposed violence as a means to make gains, to impose or to oppress. For us, every sword was double edged, and any win from cruelty would always be short lived. Yet, here was

Phillip, chasing me with nothing but a passionate anger, ferocious and naked.

I looked back to check on my head start and was relieved to see he had slowed, like he didn't fancy his chances. Martha still crouched over herself in the shallow shore, as if cradling a perfect child, bawling. I escaped over the brow of the hill and out of sight, and kept running for good measure. Damo was nowhere to be seen. I carried on running and took the back path back up to the Pile. I slipped through the commune unnoticed and found my home, my wooden hut that was always open, my cot.

I felt sheltered to be there, but it did not unbend me, in fact the fog I could not shake seemed to thicken and swirl into a twisting storm, and I grew dizzy and I fell into my bed. I lay there and through the tempest in my mind I began to see Kyra, the victim, the slaughtered lamb. I knew she had been murdered. How she used to come through my open door, always knowing she would be welcomed. My beautiful dead Kyra, my sister. When was the last time she came through that door?

And where was Damo? I needed to ask him those questions, I needed his answers. The urgency had grown, now that he had disappeared, leaving me to go to the lake like that and so covering myself with shame. I felt a sudden hatred for Martha and Phillip which deflected my disgrace, my humiliation, but not for long. I wanted to hate myself for my animal tendencies but the fog would not let me think straight, my thoughts were at the will of the storm and I had no control of what it threw out, like a hurricane blocking out the sun and tossing out cars and homes and memories. The maddened faces of Martha and Phillip span towards my minds eye, reminding me of my debased desires, total judgement. Why did I hate them so much? Was it because of Kyra?

We Journeyed together, not so long ago, Kyra and I. Here under this ample roof, the shelter I had built with my own hands, my own two shaking hands. They rattled now with all the weariness of death and I burrowed down into my bed, groaning, gasping.

We had Journeyed together and she had finally told me about what had brought her to the Pile, why she was forced to leave that miscarried civilisation she had not chosen. It was a difficult Journey for both of us, and it had taken years for her make it. We had neighboured and we sat in front of my open fire keeping each other warm, hiding each other from the naked winds quivering outside the door. Was it after this Journey that I started to feel differently about her? Was this the thing which makes my hands shake so much?

"To love a thing means wanting it to live" Kyra said to me 'Confucius' I nodded carefully in recognition of the quote, but for some reason I felt my defences raising.
'And I loved my Mother' she continued, 'I loved her so much.'
'I understand my sister' I said, sensing we were on the edge of opening a beautiful chest, full of scorpions.
'I just wanted her to live, that's all' she said, her eyes trembling.

Her beautiful eyes. When had I seem the last? This morning yes, but they were the eyes of the dead. Her beautiful dead eyes.

'I just wanted her to live. I didn't want her to leave me on my own.'

My memory let fragments appear through the fog, but hiding the whole in those greys, and those blacks.

'She was sick. It got her badly. She knew she didn't have long left.'
'Don't cry, don't cry my sweet.'

I love her so much. I loved her so much. My hands still shake guiltily, the fog won't let me remember.

'I loved Mother so I kept her alive. I knew if she went to the hospital that she wouldn't come back. First her legs stopped working, then her arms and her hands.'

My hands.

'Then her speech left her. She was leaving me quickly and I could see it in her failing eyes. She tried to say goodbye but I wouldn't let her.'

Oh Kyra what did you do? What did I do?

'She didn't want to eat, or her mouth wouldn't let her. But I put a tube down her throat and mushed up all her favourites, bangers and mash, fish and chips, even Sunday dinner.'

She wasn't right in the head. I realised that. I found out. I knew all along.

'Then she stopped breathing. No matter though, I made a ventilator and a mask which kept her lungs going, breathing in and out, her chest going up and down, she was still alive if she was breathing.'

She was crazy. I knew it, I knew it.

'Her body got stiff but I changed her clothes and bedsheets everyday. Her skin went funny coloured so I used creams and make up to patch her up, and I kept

pumping her with the ventilator bag. Up
and down, up and down, breathing, alive.'

A psychopath.

'She was very very sick and the smell of
disease kept growing in the air so I used
perfume to hide the stench. She was too
sick for visitors, I looked after her with
24hour care, keeping her breathing,
pumping. I slept in her bed with her,
cuddling her like she cuddled me as a
child, keeping her warm. She was so cold.'

Wrong. Fundamentally bad. Evil? You knew
you couldn't trust her.

'I spent all day fighting the insects and
keeping her fed and pumped and clean and
looking pretty. It was exhausting. I held
her tightly, wishing she could grip me
back, imagining the thud of her beating
heart against mine. I held her tight till
the bad men came.'

No you love her. Loved her. You had no
right to judge. You're not the police
anymore.

'The bad men came but I ran away. To love
a thing means wanting it to live.'

Your hands. Your love.

```
I snuggled down into my cot of hay and
pulled my blanket completely over my body
and face. I felt a desire to hide, an
innate retreat, to dissolve into  my
primordial guts and be invisible. I wanted
to run away.
```

I knew where she'd be. And she knew I'd know. That's what she wanted, for me to chase her, to head out into the close steamy night. She'd be sitting in the pub. Not our pub, not the pub we had our first drinks in (we had called it drinks, not a date), not the pub where we knew all the numbers for our favourite songs on the jukebox, not the pub where we first kissed in the beer garden, our tongues working each other out, settling into their new grooves.

She'd be in the other pub, her pub, where the drinks are too expensive for my taste and where her ex-boyfriend seems to constantly work, with his famous posture, his perma-grin and his knowing winks. That's where she'll be, leaning on the bar like a little girl in the sweet shop.

Weakness had opened the door, let her into my thoughts, let her get to me. I had to go and find her now, so I reluctantly left my desk. I should have turned on the television or listened to the radio or something. But instead I thought about the pet rats

I had as a kid. I should have checked my phone or looked out of the window or something. But my rats had returned to me and it felt fitting to think about them, as I dug out my trainers and double checked my pockets. Phone Keys Wallet Rats.

Martha and Phillip were what they were named. I had stolen their names from my memory for the characters in my story. Martha and Phillip, even though they were both boys. I had chosen the names seemingly at random from a childhood book, resolutely pointing with grubby fingers and declaring the baptism. And I clearly still hold onto them now.

Martha and Phillip lived in a cage sat on a set of drawers in my room. My room with the dinosaurs on the wall, iguanodon and triceratops posing between the floating adhesive heads of Matt le Tissier, Eric Cantona and Gareth Southgate. A discouraged crayon graffito rested nearby, as Martha and Phillip scuttled from storey to storey in their transpicuous little house.

One day I put my finger through the bars in the cage. Martha, the rat, leapt from the sawdust and sunk his teeth into the top of my wrinkly digit, pouncing like a cobra and sinking his sharp yellow teeth into my skin. He gripped on as I screamed and tried to pull my finger back out of the cage, but his jaws were tight and he was stubbornly gnawing. When I wrenched it back through he had taken a terrifying chunk, and the blood was dripping down onto my pyjamas. The pain seemed numbed by some morbid fascination for my freshly mangled finger, as I held it up the light and examined the glistening mutilation.

The vacuum cleaner moaned away downstairs and Ma had not heard my yelp. I thought about running now, tumbling down the stairs, holding my damaged finger like a torch, imploring some Motherly pity. But Martha had my attention once again, with my blood on his whiskers, and my skin on his crooked teeth, and him running around the cage, round and round and up and down those noisy ladders. He had the taste of blood with him now, the ravenous lust of the madman impeding his rodent brain. He was utterly crazed and Phillip cowered in the corner of the cage, possibly more aware of his confinement then he ever had been before.

Martha leapt from wall to wall, huffing and wheezing and squealing and almost howling like a rabid wolf at the height of some furious infection. He intoxicated my ten year old eyes. My injured finger still throbbed away at my side, the blood maybe clotting, maybe still dripping on my socks and leaving its vermilion reminders on the carpet.

And I watched as he set on poor Phillip. I watched as he forced himself onto his cage mate, sinking his teeth into his neck and scrabbling upon his back as if trying to find some grip with his vile spikes of claws. I watched him dig his teeth deeper into Phillips rat neck and the blood growing thick in the fur and the life leaving Phillips eyes as Martha humped on his back, in what I later learned was a stab for his anus. Not that he would have felt that indignant pain, he was choking on his own blood in his punctured throat as Martha gnawed and bucked and scratched and killed. Phillips fur slipped away from his jaw and his eye sockets revealing what the frenzied Martha was lasciviously chewing on. He wasn't Phillip anymore.

Even in my unbloomed mind, I felt the cage was an appropriate place for that bloodlust. And so I picked it up at its base, struggling with its weight and the unhinged scene inside,

Martha once again bouncing from wall to wall, trying to tear my hands which I kept on the plastic bottom. Phillips abject rat corpse slid around the base, leaving a wretched slime as it went. I climbed onto a chair placed by the open window and launched the murderer and his cell and his victim into the abyss of the garden. I watched as the cage hurtled downwards to the cement hexagons of the patio, spinning in some slow motion justice, and then crashing into its constituent parts.

I saw a blood soaked blob dash away from the wreckage and run for the bins. Martha had escaped my assassination attempt, my first bid for justice, recompense, revenge, whatever you want to call it. He had gotten away with it. I thought I was saying bye bye to Martha forever, but apparently I was not.

I opened the front door and was hit with the smell of burning rubber in the night air, yanking me back to the present, and whatever reality it offered. The air had weight and volume and that hot turd stench. I felt blessed to have left my joint upstairs, as there was already enough trouble in that dank dangerous fug. I set off for the pub with caution.

I turned the corner and was met by a screen of heat and light, the blinding lick forcing me a step back as I figured out the shape in the flames. It looked like the neighbours Corsa, the chassis bending in the fire and melting. A Punto sat flipped onto its warped roof further ahead, and several more cars which lined the road were aflame, lighting the road up to the pub like bonfires, blazing signals and the warning signs of attack.

A blue light illuminated the side of some houses at the top of the street, a flailing cerulean gleam, a flashing light with no sign of the siren. Not that there was silence. Car alarm, house alarm, shop alarm all bleated on in verbose cacophony. The police chopper circled somewhere in the near above, searching down with its Sauron eye, an audible menace.

I thought I could hear shouting over the helico blades, down one of those undesirable tributaries. The street lights were turned off down a few of them, but I wasn't going to go search out the din. I aimed myself for the pub instead, and for her.

The noise of various sirens, police, ambulance, fire all whizzed through the air, speeding around the neighbourhoods of neighbours. But not this one. I started to worry about her. What had become of her in this urban chaos? Why did she have to run away? I hoped to the heavens that she had made it to the pub, surely this madness would not encroach on that most holiest of sanctums.

I could see no people amidst the carnage, no cops or robbers, no zombie horde, just a sensation of eyes peeking out behind curtains, hiding behind the shrill caveat of the alarm orchestra. I passed an overturned Clio further up the tortured street, and that's when I started to jog, spurned on by the havoc and the unreal. I ran past more car and wheelie bin pyres, over a sea of smashed glass, clear, green, amber, red, like urban sea shells thick and thin. Every parked car that wasn't on fire had it's windows caved in or out.

And I had the pub in my sights as I felt that flailing cerulean gleam coming up behind me, the police siren wailing, deafening at it dopplered past, as full pelt as the frontline required. Then the scorched screech of emergency braking, and a seamless shift to that noise of a car engine in full on reverse, one of the most ominous of noises there is. Plod stopped again just in front of me, checking me out in his mirrors, as I stood still. I hate police as much as the next good man, but I've never been one for wanting trouble. Fortunately, I wasn't the one he wanted me to be and he fucked off at full pelt once again, screaming round the corner and out of sight. I took the final sprint to the pub, desperate to see her in where I thought she'd be.

```
It was last night. She walked through that
door last night. Revelations attack me
through the fog, as I hide under my
blanket, the hay scratching my neck as it
sinks into my shoulders, my knees coming
up to my chest and cuddled by still
shaking hands.

The story of her Mother had unsettled me,
rattled me like my rattling hands, thrown
me off the bridge and into the tumultuous
water below. But I know there was more to
it than that.

You know there was more to it than that.

The conversation unravelled into my
consciousness, the next Journey we took
```

that night. Last night. It came at me again through the fog.

'I don't think we should be Neighbours anymore' she told me, distancing her body from mine, 'This needs to stop'.

I remember the distant rumbling of loneliness far away, like a quick fire on the Savanna horizon.

'I don't understand.'

I remember that old lonely feeling creeping up on me, being turfed out in the cold once again, alone with my appalling self.

'I don't feel free,' she said, 'isn't that the point of being at the Pile?'

I remember it warping my spine, tickling my neck, making me shudder.

'What are you saying?' 'Why are you doing this to me?'

I remember falling into a big black hole.

'Well ... I've been talking to Martha and Phillip, and Damo ...'

Damo.

'What about Damo?' I said back through gritted teeth.

'Damo? What do you mean?'
'WHAT ABOUT DAMO?' I screamed back 'WHAT ABOUT DAMO?'
'I don't ... I don't understand.'
'WHAT ABOUT FUCKING DAMO?'
'I'm sorry, I'm sorry, I'm sorry' she cowered.

There's a knock on the door, someone's outside. Another knock and shouting too. It seems a lot of people are outside. Let me hide here some more, under these warm blankets.

What the fuck are you doing here? she asks, wide eyed. It's not the sweet shop picture I imagined, more a scene of pre-emptive survival, as if that pub door I burst through was just about to be locked. That cunt behind the bar gives me his famous nod, no canny grin tonight though. She charges over to meet me with those eyes, burning like the streets outside.

I came looking for you, I said, I was worried about you.
Well I wish you didn't she stroked back, shepherding me away from the gathered crowd of survivalists.
They're fucking rioting. A full blown riot. The cops shot some guy and now it's all kicked off. It's crazy out there.

I know, I know, I saw.
Why did you come?

Why did I come? I looked at the sticky carpet, its brothel reds and its greasy blacks. Why did I come? Maybe I'm just following the masculine narrative, always seeking closure.

What do you want?
I want to chat.
What's to say? You were a dick back there.
Why do you always run away?
Why not? There's no point fighting.
We're not fighting.
We fucking are.

I saw a blackened stubborn chud stuck in that carpet and it became all I could see.

I'm not happy. You're not happy. We're not happy. That's all there is to it. She spelt it out.

I grasped at something made of mist.
What do you mean happy?
I'm not fucking happy, that's what I mean.
But happiness is fleeting. It's not something we can capture and keep forever.
Oh here we go.
It's a symptom, a neat syndrome that shows us where we're going. A chemical pointer for progress. If A is unhappiness, it doesn't make B happiness, it's the line that joins them, the journey, and …
She cut me off with her eyes and waited that killer second

before flooring me once again. What the fuck am I supposed to say back to that?

I had no answer. My eyes went back to the crusty stained chewing gum, the carpet looked like lava and felt like quicksand.

This is exactly it, I'm trying to talk about us, about me and about you, but all you come out with are these pathetic pseudo-bullshit diatribes. You're always hiding behind something.
Like what?
My god, your job for one. You hide behind it constantly. You hate it, you've hated it since your first day there for fucks sake. If you hate it so much why are you still working there? It makes no sense.
I do it for us, for the flat. It's a bad time to be out of work, you know that.
Yes I do know that thank you! But I'm trying to do what I want to do, to follow my dreams. Why don't you follow yours instead of making excuses all the time? If you want to be a fucking writer, quit your fucking job!
It's nearly finished, it's nearly there.
I'm sick of hearing about it. You always complain that you've got no time to write, and then you sit down and smoke weed and fall asleep listening to that record, The Dark Side of the Moon. You always play that fucking record. The same shit over and over again, round and round. Fitting really.

My dreams. Follow My dreams. Damo. Where was he taking me?

You're a passenger on a journey you didn't even choose. You have no control over your life and it seems to me you don't

even want any. I need someone who knows what they want.
Knows how to get it. Knows Nose Noise Noise Noise.

The chud seems to grow and grow and it's not a chud at all it's
a big black hole, swallowing, engulfing me, pulling me to its
impossible bottom, drowning me because it's tar and it sticks
in my mouth and clogs up my throat and I can't breathe and
I'm dying.

She's still talking. We've both changed. I think we both know
that deep down. It has ran its course. We can still be friends.
It's over. That kind of thing.

It's fucking over.

I think about getting angry but I know she's the one talking
sense.

She's never been so right.

I notice the cunt behind the bar is keeping a beady eye on
proceedings as he systematically dries a pint glass. I notice her
saying sorry and are you ok. I notice the brick coming through
the red and green stained glass window. I did not jump or
scream like everyone else. I was staring exactly at the spot, the
point of entry, as it crashed through the pane. It seemed like the
loud arrival of fate.

The brick crashed down onto the lava carpet along with the
glass. Suddenly I could hear the sound of war outside, sirens
wailing against the urgent chatter of the mob, yet more glass
smashed and crunched, the ominous mass thuds of baton
against shield, the crackle of fireworks, or gunshots. There was

more shouting inside the pub but I was drawn to the door, and the clarity of violence outside.

You cant go out there! she screams as I pass through the portal, and do indeed go out there.
Leave him Kyra I hear from behind the bar, that cunt behind the bar.
And lock the fucking door behind him.

`They're banging on the door and they'll be coming in any second, we had no locks at the pile you see. No locks, no secrets.`

`They're looking for me, but I'm buried unseen under my blankets. I make sure my feet aren't sticking out and I hide.`

`They have come in now, shouting words the fog won't let me comprehend. Surely, it's grief that has driven me mad.`

`The grief and the fog.`

`They're getting closer, searching, still shouting.`

I'm out of the door and into the night. By the very nature of time every night is different, but most are still forgotten, the monotonous percussion of an ever dripping tap. But this one won't be forgotten, by any party.

It's fucking over.

Another bottle smashes next to me, the glass splashing against my trousers. Faceless people are running all around me, I'm walking through a fabulous skirmish. It's like I'm in a time lapse, the debris flying at a fraction of my thoughts. I ghost across the battlefield. A wounded soldier stance.

Follow My dreams. It's fucking over.

If the naysayers of my youth, that lazy generation who spend their worthless days writing off the future, if they were right, I should be thoroughly desensitised by now. But here I am.

Here we fucking are.

The smell of a community on fire, burning rubber and body politics. Were they gunshots or the pop pop pop of newsagent bought rockets? It felt like a plane crash wouldn't have brought me back to the soiled present, I'd just trudge past staring at the floor, crippled by the weight of this compulsion while the fallen 747 burnt away in the background.

Like a phantom in the regiment that he'd lost his life defending, I find myself in battle in spirit only. A jaded phantasm stalking the trenches, a lost visitor to this impromptu campaign, on the frontline of some crusade traversing the no mans land between black and white, dark and light. But I'm no participant.

You're a passenger on a journey you didn't even choose.

Bottles fly past me, half of which are on fire, the resourceful Molotov cocktail winged with adroit poetry. A rock or another brick skims the back of my head. I'm staring at the floor, traipsing, simply waiting for that hit once again. The light from the police bird illuminates me like a fairground target, but still I stare at that tarmac. The noises of war are all around but life's too shit to listen.

It doesn't matter if you see the car coming or not, it will always wipe you out, break you in two or send you flying over the bonnet. My life had been reduced, drained of fluid and reason. I would have vomited if I wasn't so fucking hollow, as empty as this world we've somehow found ourselves in.

She's right. She's always right. And nothing lasts forever. And nothing is forever. And maybe I've just got what I told myself I wanted and

And.

And shit. This is a fucking riot.

I snap out of it as a grenade spins out of the blackness and into my path, it fizzes out a thick black smoke. The fog. I need to get out of here, and quick. I duck just in time as some form of slab flies over me. I felt there was more to come hurtling from the darkness. Awareness had thrashed me with it's driving whip, and it seemed like those noises of war had hit the right frequency.

I sprinted in the instinctive direction of home, spooked by the fizz and fog of that grenade. Some missile crashed into my shoulder, a rock or stone I think. It nearly sent me tumbling but I kept on my feet and it served to spur me on.

I got lucky and slipped down a tight alley. I thought I was escaping the fog and the ammunition, and whatever else the darkness held, hitting another alley past the garages and then the underpass which came out by the offy and the bookies and the Tesco express. Alarms still rang out but I could hear the battle was far away enough for now, and my road was just around the corner.

As I passed the Tesco, still legging it, two short figures emerge from an opening of broken glass. As I passed I recognised my neighbours little fat kids, their dark black faces poking out under hoods, their eyes and teeth painted yellow by the glow of the street lamp. Their arms were full of looted goodies.
Fair play. Grab a few tinnies for me I shouted, but they were fittingly frigid. They probably didn't even have a clue who I was.

I flee the commercial parade and turn the corner onto my road, unaware of doom lurking around the bend. The car came from the other direction this time, but it still obliterated what was left.

Here I met the stark design of law and order, the gloomy tendrils of Moloch; Plod en masse. A dense black swarm ahead of me. Rows and rows of troops, police after police after police. All masked with shining helmets, and banging their batons against their shields as they marched forward with all the thunder of the army they thought they were. A bevy of armoured vans pushed the regiment forward with the rally of their flashing lights, and a water cannon trundled and twisted in the centre of it all, like the unruly behemoth troll drafted and chained.

My problem was that their formidable line now blocked me from the front door of my flat.

Our flat.

Where we lost ourselves in late night conversation. Where we scrubbed each others backs in the bath. Where we made each other breakfast in bed. Where we had our private jokes and our burping competitions. Where we made love by the light of a candle. Where we spent come-down Sundays watching shit films and drinking bloody mary's. Where had all those times gone? What the fuck had even happened?

I thought about running away. Away from the pain and the riot cops, somehow gaining remedy from the business of feet, from spontaneous flight. But I thought No, this is my road. That is my flat. Those are my dreams.

I was suddenly full of the most potent of angers, a love fuelled apoplexy, full of haste, full of reckless hate. I was ruled by sweet passion and mania. It was time to stop being a passenger.

YOU! GET OUT OF THE WAY GET OUT OF THE WAY megaphoned a voice from the dark mass.
That's my house! I pleaded, pointing, knowing I was unheard under the helicopters and the alarms and the sirens.
STAND BACK I REPEAT STAND BACK as I fully see the water cannon tank behind the cadre. I stood my ground but the wall seemed to be accelerating towards me.
DISPERSE I REPEAT DISPERSE as I feel the juggernaut stupefaction of a tidal wave, an unstoppable trance that only gets taller.
THIS IS YOUR LAST WARNING
But my house! My house! That's my house! My ...

I don't feel the lightning punch, the breakneck hammer to my chest. It's only when I'm down on the floor, my lungs paralysed, not only breathless but somehow drowning as if in a vacuum. I'd been shot, taken out, whacked. I was down and I thought I was out but something still wanted to go on inside me, the pain maybe, and I found myself somehow back on one knee, mounting one last impossible stand, one last shot at life. All I needed to do was get back on two feet and

That's when I felt the chemical burn in my eyes, a searing fire disject. I'm back on the floor, writhing, rolling, my fingers trying to remove my scorched eyes from their sockets. I can only see white hot pain, but I hear many feet and hostile shuffling. I try to get up again, to retreat to escape from this torrid blind hell. I just needed to get out of here and

That's when the truncheons rained down upon me. Stick after hard metal stick after stick after stick after evil wretched stick. First my arms and ribs and wounded chest and then my legs and my feet and my cock and my hands and my fingers and my burning face and

finally my head.

There was a light. A light so white and welcoming and warm. That's where we were heading, in our little boat, summoned into the lights gracious embrace.

And that light now flooded into the tunnel, chasing our lamp to redundancy. I could now see the whole of the tunnel we were leaving, a structure of thousands of thick twisted roots. Our soundtrack took on a new acoustic quality as we left the confines of the tunnel, and what it lost in closeness it gained in clarity, as if we had been graced with a cinematic soundtrack. It filled the close air of the mighty Amazonian rainforest in which we now found ourselves.

The stream had filtered into a pool in which we were now bobbing, surrounded by these sky-scraping trees as giant as they were ancient. The canopy hung ominously above, thick like rainclouds, so that if you were flying above them you would not see the pond and boat hidden below. Damo rowed ashore at the first clearing, pointing the boat and then jumping out to finish the job with his arms and rope. I still stood in the boat staring up at this fresh ceiling. I saw shafts of light searching through the canopy, occasionally going the distance. I felt a humidity I had never felt before, and the sweat on my back and temples felt real.

Floyd still grooved on through the old trees above, echoing off giant trunks and swimming through swarms of leaves, but its presence was very nearly matched by the dense dialogue of the rainforest, the howls and jabberings, the squawks and chatter from millions of invisible mouths, hidden within imperceptible vicinities.

The life within the forest and the forest itself felt like an institution in its worldly authority, as if it were a place for all answers and secrets. And like all institutions it invoked mistrust, seeing in the shady dealings of the leaves and limbs above that there's no love lost for the little man. And I had never felt so little as I did gawping up at these giants, now willing to follow my still silent guide into the undergrowth.

A blue-arsed fly the size and weight of a squash ball collided into the side of my face and then buzzed away into the sweat of the forest. Damo had drawn a machete from beneath his trench coat and began to scythe a path forward through the bush. I followed closely behind, brushing away vines and branches as they lunged down to grab at my face.

- Do you know where we're going? he shouted back over his shoulder.

He had finally broken the silence, but I knew I could not reply.

- Of course you don't. You're a passenger on a journey you didn't even choose.

Damo worked away at the age old thicket with cruelty, the machete raining down like an overseers whip, and other tools of progress. Progress however was made slowly here, the forest constricting with every yard conquered. Damo sliced on and on and I winced in his shadow, the forest seemingly closing up behind us as we trudged through, the machete inflicting but a scratch.

- We're going hunting.

I knew I had no choice other than to accept that was what we were doing here in this sweltering breathing place.

- We're going to kill something.

Still he spoke to me from over his shoulder.

- Something very special.

He continued to shave our path forward with his rugged knife, the chops and churns a rhythmic compliment to the celestial organ of Us and Them.

- We are going to eat it. We are going to end it.

He turned to face me as he finished the sentence. His face was as grim as bile.

- An end awaits us all and everything else too. It isn't so hard when you see it coming.

I thought it doesn't matter if you see it coming or not, it's still going to chop you in half.

- Well you're wrong.

Wait. He can read my thoughts.

- Of course I can. And death can only be in front of us.

He stopped suddenly as if ready to pounce, instructing me to freeze with his upturned palm. The palm turned to a stern finger to his creased limps, silencing me prone. We waited there a second, him scanning the canopy above, me scanning my guide and captor. It looked like we'd missed our chance, but of what I did not know. He continued on into the rainforest, and I dutifully followed.

- Death is irrelevant to time. Time does not care whether you are dead or alive, or whether you are unborn.

I was struggling to keep up.

- Try harder then. Time is not bothered by existence, it has its own less trivial agenda. It is existence who cherishes time, needs it for its narratives, worships at its altar. As you might put it, time is existences guide and captor.

He looked at me again as he said it, his face made dire with menace under his wide brimmed hat.

- But death can still inspire. An impetus for the living, anyway. Death is only for the living. The dead don't know about death, and the lucky ones don't know about dying.

He shushed me again with his hand, and then began to charm a thin long stick from the sleeve of his trench coat. It looked like bamboo and he pulled it from nowhere with Mary Poppins magic. He found a rudimentary dart in his pocket, decorated with exquisite feathers, and placed it into the wooden chamber. He took aim somewhere high in the canopy, at what I didn't have the eyes to see. He put the end to his mouth and blew a short sharp thump from his blowgun.

- Gotcha.

I still could not see what it was, but after a few seconds of relative silence I heard the breaking of branches high in the covering. Something had begun its descent, and by the sounds of the snaps and cracks it was something big.

- An end awaits us all.

The thing boomed onto the forest floor somewhere close and Damo jumped into action, scything his way towards the fallen body. I kept chase, leaping through the bush which did its best to trip me.

- Here.

Now I could see our game, lying there crooked on the ground. She was an orang-utan, beautiful, young, perverted forever from her arboreal berth. She still clung to life, twitching.

- Good night my sister.

He took a smaller sharper blade from his belt and took it to her throat. The saxophone played on.

Floyd was our hypnagogic companion as we made ourselves a clearing and built ourselves a fire. I stared a long while at the beautiful dead ape, she had a little bald patch atop her handsome face and dark delicate eyes. Her lips were flaccid and pointed to her emptied throat, sullied by the blood in her familiar hair. Damo soon had her prepared for the fire. I did not feel hungry and I did not feel sick. I was beginning to not feel anything at all.

It seemed like he hadn't said another word to me until we sat there, the primate roasting over the lick of the flames. He snapped off one her long crispy arms and threw it into my lap. Her scorched hand flapped over my thigh. The fingers looked so real.

- Eat, he said. Now she is immortal.

I bit off a chunk in the centre of the forearm. It tasted like plague.

- Anyone who has tasted existence has a rite to immortality. Life is there for us to earn it.

I chewed the disgusting meat round and round in my mouth, unable to get it down. I felt suddenly on edge as Damo gave me a disturbing smile, his teeth littered with the orang-utan flesh.

- Relax, he said. His creepy mouth full, chewing wide open.

I thought I saw a snake flick past my ankles, a thick green grass snake sliding through the leaves. I jumped up from my perch and dropped the ruined arm to the floor and spat out what I couldn't swallow. I swore I saw something. Something thick and long rustled under the leaves very closely. I felt something brush past my leg and disappear beneath the foliage. I didn't understand what was happening.

- What's to understand? All the understanding we need is right here. You might learn something if you let yourself.

I saw the snake once again rushing through the vegetation. To my horror I saw that there was two of them, certainly moving faster then they should, somehow circling me. What horrible lesson was this? What was the point?

- The point is that everything must come to an end.

I felt something grip me tight round both ankles simultaneously and whisk me straight to the decaying floor. I wallowed there a second, looking at Damo for help and for answers, but he just laughed a manic laugh, his mouth even fuller than before.

- Go find immortality! Good night my brother!

And then I felt a great tug at my ankles, pulling me away from the fire and him still laughing and chewing and laughing. I tried to grab on to something but everything to hand was dead or dying, except for the long arms which had lassoed me, now dragging me through the sharp undergrowth, cutting my face and hands. I managed to turn round slightly to see where I was headed and saw the two thick green arms, jungle vines, coiled around my ankles. I tried to punch one but it did not flinch, instead pulling harder making me as helpless as a fish on a line. I truly began to panic when I saw what the fisherman looked like.

I was being dragged to a clandestine clearing in the rainforest. There, with many other jungle vine arms waving in the air, like tentacles, was a venus fly trap as huge as it was ferocious. Roughly the size and bulk of a large elephant, it snapped its huge mouth open and shut, the huge mouth which was all it was, except for its vine tentacles which waggled with anticipation all around it, two of which still had a perfect grip on its prey. Its terrible uncountable teeth interlocked with grim precision as it snapped open again and again, making a terrible din like a crocodile chomping air. Suddenly I was in the air, more vine arms now had a hold of me, and I was looking down into the snapping mouth of the carnivorous plant monster.

The venus man trap seemed to be toying with his find, tossing me from tentacle to tentacle, hovering me over his green lips, I even thought I saw it salivating. The fact I could see no throat, no tonsils at the back of the vile berth, filled him with even more terror, I knew of the cruel and unusual methods of these meat eaters.

And as the final slow descent into the mouth of the monstrous plant began, I could only stare into the dungeon of digestion which awaited me, so frozen by fear and the futility of my struggling, still utterly crippled by silence. The last chords of Brain Damage faded away as I was plopped into my sticky coffin, immediately glued into place without hope of escape. I thought I heard voices, voices and laughter that reminded me of home, so far far away from here.

And then sssnnnaaappp.

The mouth that was the plant   clamped   shut

and   dark   ness.

    And   Eclipse.

REST

'Here! Here he is!'
The voices bellow like thunder to the ancients, a terrifying reminder of hell. I feel the blanket whisked from my curled up body. I am exposed but my eyes remained sealed.

If I can't see them.

They can't see me.

I'm awake. I know that I am awake. I want to pull the tubes from my nose as soon as I realise they're up there, the nasty conduits drive right into my torpid brain, and I can hear the nurse dancing with the machines. But the lids on my eyes are drawn to the molten centre of the earth and the pure chaos of it's subterranean nightmare, keeping us all together, a planet within a planet.

They don't know if it was the rubber bullet or the truncheons which broke all these ribs. They say it was miraculous that my lungs survived. The pepper spray no longer stings, but the wires in my jaw make my face throb when the morphine runs out. I just press a button though, and then it comes back.

It's been really helpful for my writing, has lovely lady M. Now that I have chance to finish what I started, to put an ending to my story, prone here in this hospital bed. My fingers won't type without the morphine, I click the switch and I drift off into the deepness of my recesses. The words seem to look after themselves, touching each other up and making friends.

I click the switch and wait to see if my newly crooked fingers will spur into action. My eyes roll back in my head and I struggle with my eyelids once again, before my gaze falls upon beautiful flowers and the wondrous cavities of my bedside desk. There's a thick book there too that I'm reading, and I see the promotional quote on its cover:

"An intellectual adventure story, as sensational, thrilling, and packed with arcana as Raiders of the Lost Ark or The Count of Monte Cristo" - The Washington Post Book World

Isn't that where we live now? A post book world? The morphine makes me see everything clearer, as long as it's the size of a keyhole.

'Here! Here he is!'
'Get him up!'
'Open your eyes. Open your eyes now, my so called brother!'

I can't ignore the voices anymore. It feels like the loud arrival of fate. I open my eyes at their command, and see the mob all around me. It seems like the whole of the Pile has come to see me. Martha and Phillip are at the vanguard, with fury in their judgmental faces.

'You bastard' Martha hisses. I don't seem to possess the energy to answer back.

'What have you got to say for yourself?' asks one of the elders, but I can't seem to answer his question either.

'We found you with her there this morning, but we kept quiet until we could figure out a way to put the pieces together' says Phillip, addressing both me and everyone else in the room, 'We found you there this morning by the lake with her body.'

'No, the fog. No.' I utter but I'm too quiet to be heard, 'I found you there, I found you.'

'Why did you do it?' chimes Martha again, 'Why? Was it because she wanted to leave you? She told us you were possessive, she told us she was scared of you.'

The fog finally began to lift as I rubbed my temples with my hands, my wide eyes now staring at the floor. I tried to summon some defence and the fog seemed to relent with every fresh accusation, the words burning it away like the mid morning Sun.

'Did you do it? Did you take her away from us?'

'No. No. Please stop, please.'

'You're just another violent bent copper, you've never been one of us.'

'No it's not true. It can't be true'

'Why were you so eager to put her body on the fire? To turn her mortal soul to ash?'

'No. Not me, not me.'

As the impeachments raged forward the fog continued to thin. I looked up and scanned the blurry clump of acrimonious faces which circled me, looking for Damo. He was not there. With the acquiesce of the fog my cognition was returning, but as I looked for the face of Damo I began to realise I could not recall it. No features or mug mien sprang to mind, just a blank pink orb somehow familiar. It felt like he was leaving with the fog, as if he needed it to survive.

'You're the only suspect. We needed today to make sure, but you made our minds up for us when you returned to the scene of the crime just hours later, where me and Martha were consoling each other down in the lake. There you returned, with your penis in your hand! Masturbating! You're sick, you're a sick pervert!'

'And a murderer!'

'No no please, it was Damo, he said it would be fine, we're all neighbours here'

I pleaded hard as the fog began to disappear and I could finally begin to comprehend my desperate situation. I was beginning to see again, my thoughts and memories returning, yet I longed for blindness.

'Damo made me do it.'

'What do you mean, Damo?' someone asked.

'Damo made me do it,' I sniffed back, my head now fully in my hands, hiding once again, 'Damo made me do it.'

Now the fog has left and I'm there for all to see, revealed like a corpse hidden by a long frozen winter, exposed by the change of seasons and the ruthless arrow of time. There was a short silence, and some muffled gasps. I am an animal on display.

I hear the words 'Crazy' and 'Lost it' whispered and floated through the air. An elder comes close and brings himself down to my level, to address me and to look into my tired eyes.

'I see. But you are Damo, there is no other here at the Pile by that name. Your name is Damo. Do you understand?' he said calmly.

I am unveiled. I know this to be true, now the fog has let me see. To see is to understand and I much preferred my ignorance.

'You're Damo, you were a police officer. Your son was murdered and you came here to us, to our colony. Do you not remember?'

I did remember. Finally, I remember. I remember but I don't want to remember. I want it to be yesterday. I give my persecutors a sombre nod.

'And do you remember what happened with our sister Kyra? She was seen coming to your home last night, and you were found with her flown body this morning. It does not look good Damo, it looks very bad indeed.'

I crave the fog. I want the fog to engulf me again, and to make me blind. Make me forget.

'Where's the fog?' I mumble.

'You bastard!' hisses Martha again with venom and tears in her eyes, 'You horrible fucking bastard'.

I nod again. The fog isn't coming to save me, only the clear vision of fresh tortured memories.

The jealousy.

'I'm sorry.' I cry.

Alone again.

'I'm so sorry.'

My hands around her neck.

'I'm so fucking sorry.'

The scene descends into uproar and I bury my head into my shaking hands. I hear screams and shouting. Many bodies rush around but I am frozen.

Finally I am hoisted to my feet. I am dragged from my nest. I do not resist, but I keep my head in my hands, hiding from the shouting and the insults that are being thrown at me. I feel spit and wet mud thrown at me.

I hear the drums and see the pyre lit up once again, the cleansing flame crackling into the sky for the second time that day.

I can walk now, but I prefer to do my thinking lying down, staring up at the panels of the ceiling, wondering how many people had had the same view as they slipped into death. And I've had a lot of time to think. Time to reflect on what went wrong, and how it came to be. How I had let it all turn to shit.

So, he was Damo after all. He was the killer, he was the one who had ended it all. He had solved his own mystery, and everything was his fault. He was looking for someone else to blame all along. I thought that sounded familiar.

I wonder what she would think of that whodunit ending. Contrived? Disingenuous? Convoluted? Bullshit? She's probably right, but I'm starting to think it's best to not care what she thinks anymore. That would be the first step on this lonely road, not looking back and learning to live with myself once again.

The riot had been buried by the worlds continual supply of news, consigned to a night to forget for everyone but me.

Had she come to visit when I was out cold? I looked at the well wishing cards next to me for what seemed like the first time, as if they belonged to the beds previous occupier who might not have made it out alive; Get well soon. Hang in there buddy. Wishing you a swift recovery. A multitude of Clintons concern. And then there's one from her:

Dear Damo,

So sorry to hear about what happened.

We may have drifted apart but I'll always be here for you.

Let's chat when you're better.

Kyra x

I had pushed her away. Took her for granted, while I hid behind the things that didn't matter; shit jobs, shit rent, shit habits. My shame. I blamed her for my own discrepancies, and cowered behind my many excuses. I had wished it to be over so many times, I can't now act the victim. I can see this now I've had this little break, or several of them around my broken body. I can see this now the fog has cleared, and I've worked out my own charade.

I put my headphones back in and resume my escape, music being my only way off this stinking ward now they've taken away my morphine. Through the window the last of the summer days are teasing into a cool brisk evening, but I can only dream of rolling a tight joint and sitting under that tree or on that bench, the lukewarm rays coaxing a smile from my face.

I was the one who had ran away, not her. Ran away into my stories and my pained metaphors. I was the one who found far too much refuge in the sofa and and my anodyne dreams. But when you refuse to live in the present, when you accept that you're a passenger whisked between the past and the future and accepting nothing in between, stubbornly rejecting Now, how can you see what you're truly doing? Only through my sentence, my enforced reflection, can I now see through all that fog.

It's always too late of course. It's like we can only look at something after we've climbed out of it, or fallen out of its bottom, been shit out. We can write our letters, make our pleas, enslave ourselves to the perpetual dodge of loneliness and its drowning dunks, an infinite baptism. But where actions speak louder than words, it is actions, or lack of them, which become the iconic speeches, the chimerical idols of the longing past.

And just because we're outside of something and can see it from all angles doesn't mean we're in control. In fact it's like being chucked off a space station and floating off forever into the darkness of space, as your shining home hurtles onwards, unreachable, flying forwards on its unstoppable orbit.

It's almost as if the only thing is to change, to come through the blackness a better person, to show despair for the desperate fool he is. Change can only be a good thing, time demands that be our only truth. Change can help us break, it can help us fix, and it can help us unmask.

I've never seen the point of doing laps or the treadmill. When I run I want to run away, somehow to escape. And although that's something I want to change, it seems elemental to my character, inborn and it's even helping me now, making it easy to move forward, wherever that may be. Maybe I need someone to run away with me. Maybe that's what I already had but couldn't see through that fog.

I jump out of my thoughts as I feel a hand on my shoulder which startles me. I peel my eyes from the window to see who it belongs to. It's the nurse, and I look up at her, and her face reflects the beautiful light outdoors which had me so enraptured. Was she new here? I pull the phones from my ears with my unbroken arm.

What are you listening to? she asks.
The Dark Side I say.
SO overrated, she cuts me off before I can say Of the Moon.
I notice that smile for the first time and those eyes, both mischievous and maternal. I liked her.
You're not into The Dark Side of the Moon?
It's OK, I just don't get why it's the go-to psychedelic reference point for everyone, you know?
Yeah, I guess so. I think about my dream and how it hadn't returned since the blackness. I watch her faff at the end of the bed. I really liked her. So, what's your favourite Floyd album then?
You do know it's 2011 right?
Was I in a coma for that long? I attempt to joke.
I'm surprised by the laughter it garners out of her. Are we flirting here? Or is it just pity? Either way I feel alive again.

But if you're asking, I guess it's Animals she says as she reads my file rather absently.
Oh yeah? Very Orwellian.
Yeah. If you think about it, we're all Pigs, Dogs or Sheep aren't we?
We're animals alright, that's for sure.
I look to the window once again, but only for some sort of dramatic pretence, which she seems keen to dismiss.
Yeah we're apes, I get it, great apes.
Apparently so.
Did you know Bonobos are the only other animal which have sex face to face?

For some reason I blush and give a flustered giggle.

Do you know if a girl has come to see me? I ask as she does something to the bed and the sheets.
You mean when you were in intensive care?
Yep.
I don't think so. Your parents came everyday, but you were so keen on that Morphine you weren't making much sense for a while. But it should be out of your system now.
Tell me about it I say, with a wink, and it's her turn to emit a knowing giggle.
I'd say she's about my age.

She stops her work and sits down on the low slouched seat near my bed, and applies a face of gorgeous concern.
So. Who's this girl then?
Oh. Just an ex. I fight back that frantic feeling inside, but however much my head can rationalise, I have no control over this weirdness in my belly. Just an ex.
And are you still in love?
Nah, I lie. With a wince.
Love isn't that simple though right?
It really fucking isn't.
And then we both indulge in that dramatic pretence.

What about you? Are you in love? I probe to break the tiny silence.
Of course. But again, it's not so simple.
Why's that?
He's dead.
I'm sorry I say, wishing I could have summoned something less crappy.
It's OK, it's been a while now anyway, and as the cliche goes,

life does go on.
Time's a great healer.
The good ones go early.
He led a full life.
He's in a better place now.
God needed another angel.
Too far.
I'm sorry.
Stop saying that. Anyway, he went twice for me, and the second time was what helped me get to where I am now.
Why's that?
Well, it was about six months ago I lost his CD.
Was he a musician?
Nope, he was a Lithuanian.
What does that mean?
It means he was Lithuanian. He was a linguist. And he was the instructor on a CD; Teach Yourself Lithuanian.
I see.
Oh do you now? I used to listen to that CD everyday. Seriously, every day.
I can't imagine.
You can't. It was the worst time of my life. Labas. Kaip Sekasi. Atleiskite. Geros dienos. She repeated the words like a sacrament, her mantra of grief.
You kept him alive.
Maybe. Maybe I just wanted to hear his voice. Either way, I wasn't just keeping him alive. A relationship is a living thing, and I was keeping that alive too. But that stuff's not for the dead. Unless it's dead too. You know?
I think I know what you mean.
But one day, I left my bag on the bus and it was gone. He was gone. Fate had stolen him once again.

I'm sorry.
Stop saying that! Anyway, enough of all this. She's looking at my tubes now. She's close to me. I can feel her breath and it smells like summer.

They got you pretty bad didn't they.
You should see the other guy I say.

You should thank God you're still alive she said.
I don't believe in God, I tell her.
What do you believe in?
I don't know, something better than God at least.
But you believe? You believe in something?
I guess I do yes.
Well that's ok then. It means your human.

A good place to end, I think, and a good place to start again.